ING V

ood

THE WORMLING
BOOK V

The Author's Blood

JERRY B. JENKINS
CHRIS FABRY

Tyndale House Publishers, Inc., Carol Stream, Illinois

Visit Tyndale's exciting Web site for kids at cool2read.com

Also see the Web site for adults at tyndale.com

TYNDALE and Tyndale's quill logo are registered trademarks of Tyndale House Publishers, Inc.

The Wormling V: The Author's Blood

Designed by Ron Kaufmann

Edited by Lorie Popp

Published in association with the literary agency of Alive Communications, Inc., 7680 Goddard Street, Suite 200, Colorado Springs, CO 80920.

Library of Congress Cataloging-in-Publication Data

Jenkins, Jerry B.
    The Wormling V : the author's blood / Jerry B. Jenkins ; Chris Fabry.
        p. cm.
    Summary: Owen Reeder, the Wormling, faces a final battle with the Dragon, strengthened by his reading of The Book of the King and the knowledge that his friends and his very weakness can see him through his greatest challenge.
    ISBN-13: 978-1-4143-0159-4 (softcover)
    ISBN-10: 1-4143-0159-6 (softcover)
    [1. Adventure and adventurers—Fiction. 2. Conduct of life—Fiction. 3. Good and evil—Fiction. 4. Dragons—Fiction. 5. Fantasy.] I. Fabry, Chris, date. II. Title. III. Title: Wormling five. IV. Title: Author's blood.
    PZ7.J4138Wov 2008
    [Fic]—dc22   2007036549

Printed in the United States of America

14   13   12   11   10   09   08
 7   6   5   4   3   2   1

For Jason

"You don't have a soul. You are a Soul. You have a body."

C. S. Lewis

✦

"No arsenal, or no weapon in the arsenals of the world, is so
formidable as the will and moral courage of free men and women."

Ronald Reagan

✦

"If you want to make enemies, try to change something."

Woodrow Wilson

✦

"The bravest are surely those who have the clearest vision of what
is before them, glory and danger alike, and yet notwithstanding, go
out to meet it."

Thucydides

✦

"It is not often that someone comes along who is a true friend and a
good writer."

E. B. White

1
A Royal Entrance

I t was only fitting that the Queen's
sentence should be handed down
at the Castle of the Pines, her former
home, because this was where the
Dragon and his council retreated. Not
that they ran from any battle, for there
was no one to run from. Lowlanders
lay defeated in country fields. The
survivors hid, cowering.

The Dragon and his council members simply returned to the castle to
relax, belch fire, torment slaves, and
gloat about their victory over the
bedraggled army of the Wormling.

RHM, now the longest living aide
of the Dragon in history, attended to
his master's every need, be it food,

drink, or amusement. There was always amusement now and plans for more.

"Is the coliseum ready?" the Dragon said.

"Almost, sire. Your dwelling was in desperate need of repair, scorched as it was after your last assault there."

"Yes, I recall the way the people scurried about, trying to get away. Delightful. Are there enough citizens left to be the sport of our games?"

"Plenty, sire. Young and old and some in between."

"Good, good. I can't wait to watch them die in agony. Does it get any better than this?"

"Only when the Highlands are joined under your rule, sire. There will be plenty more amusement from the inhabitants there."

The Dragon's eyes shone red and his teeth glistened. "Yes," he hissed, drinking in the scene as if it were a sponge dipped in his favorite wine that he could suck on until the last bit was gone. "Is she here?" he said at last.

"She just arrived and the council has taken its place in the Hall of Meeting. Shall I announce you?"

The Dragon glanced at a stand that held a golden crown. "I shall wear that in her presence. A nice touch, don't you think?"

The council met in a vast room, which, even to an untrained eye, had once been ornate and splendid. Charred tapestries adorned the walls, murals now faded from the smoke graced either end, and from the ceiling hung colossal chandeliers. A masterpiece fashioned on the ceiling proved a stunning (though soot-covered) depiction of the Highlands, the Lowlands, and the invisible heavenly world—a crown and scepter leaning against a massive book, and the beings from these worlds kneeling, as if in worship to someone.

The council members this day, however, concentrated on the food slung about the table, goblets filled with drink, and bowls overflowing with fruits and nuts harvested from Lowlanders' farms. They chortled and told ribald stories (those we would not repeat) about their latest victories.

Only the presence of RHM at the door, clearing his throat, caused them to quiet. "It is my high honor and pleasure to present the supreme ruler, the preeminent power, who exercises decisive judgment, our king and sovereign, His Majesty, the Dragon."

As one, the council stood. Some banged their weapons on the floor, while others rapped on the table. All yelled or howled or whooped, filling the whole room with an unearthly noise.

The Dragon sashayed in, eyes shining. He preened and raised his head, sending a blast of fire toward the ceiling and further charring the picture of the crown, scepter, and book. With a wave he signaled the others to be seated and took his place on the throne at the head of the table. "Before we get to the main course," he said, chuckling, "I want reports. What of the so-called army of the Wormling?"

Slugspike rose at the other end of the table. He enjoyed such a prominent place not only because he had been appointed lead commander of the Dragon's armies but also because no one wanted to sit next to a being with such razor-sharp spines that oozed poison. Slugspike had volunteered to capture and kill the Wormling but had failed. Had the Dragon not done the job himself with his blast of fire at the White Mountain, he would have dispatched Slugspike. But, euphoric at being done with the Wormling and with victory in sight, the Dragon had restored him.

"We have paved the way for your new kingdom, sire," Slugspike said through puffy cheeks. "All the rabble has been dispatched, with the exception of a few stragglers."

"Stragglers?"

"Halflings and the like. We left them to bury the dead. We'll send a small contingent to take care of them when the job is finished."

The Dragon turned to Velvel, the vaxor head of Lowland military affairs. He had come to power after Daagn had been killed by the Dragon. "And my command to assemble near Dragon City?" (Dragon City was a massive walled compound under repair. In its center lay the coliseum.)

"It has been heeded," Velvel said. "The people seem glad to obey your imperial edict, sire, and to congregate in the valley while Dragon City is repaired. The coliseum is nearly—"

"Yes, yes, I've already heard."

"How much longer before you attack the Highlands and bring them under your subjection?" General Prufro said.

The rest nodded and grunted.

"We had to evacuate the Highlands except for a skeleton crew. When the minions of time have done their work, we will purge the Highlands—by that time, anyone still living will need canes and walkers."

"Minions of time?" someone said, laughing. "What a wonderful idea, sire."

Finally the Dragon cleared his throat and nodded to RHM, who quickly left the room. "And now the moment you've all been waiting for," the Dragon said. "I have a special treat. You have long known of our enemy and his Son. The older was killed long ago—incinerated—although we have had disturbing reports that he may have survived. The younger has surely been subdued by the attack of the minions. He went into hiding shortly before the Wormling invaded the Lowlands, and we will soon search for his body to make sure. We also have the alleged king and queen of the west in custody, and when their daughter is located in the Highlands, her blood will anoint my throne."

"What have you prepared for us?" Slugspike said, drooling.

The Dragon rose and turned.

Through the doorway walked a woman so unkempt that she looked like one with no home and no hope. Her hands were tied behind her and her head downcast.

"I present the wife of our enemy," the Dragon said, smiling.

2

Owen

Many in Owen's predicament would have quit. Against such odds, it would have been easier for him to simply crawl away and hide. How would the Dragon and his fiendish friends ever find him? However, as you will see, a hero, no matter his age or the odds against him, forges ahead and sees his quest to the end.

After the King had drawn the minions of time to himself and had plunged into an abyss, creating a hole in the basement of the B and B, and after Nicodemus, a messenger sent by the King, had spoken courageous words to Owen's heart, Owen had found a safe spot inside a room in the basement of the burned-out building. There, with the aid of a faint streetlamp that shone through the dead trees, he opened *The Book of the King*.

> When your heart is weary and your strength nearly gone, do not fret or lose sleep. Your father knows what you need every moment of the day. Do his will. Follow his directions. And do not worry about what you will do tomorrow, for the path will become clear once you get there.

Owen closed the book and fell asleep on top of it, exhausted from his trip to the Highlands. He had breached another portal—as it turned out, the third—and had discovered that Mr. Page was the King, his father. He had also discovered that his sister was Clara Secrest. And that the old woman in the back room of the shack was his future wife.

All this and much more swirled through his mind as he dreamed of the Lowlands. Watcher's face appeared before him. Then Humphrey and Erol came skipping through, singing. But soon the dream turned dark with a vision of RHM and the Dragon.

Owen awoke with a start and the word *Mother* on his tongue. Light flashed behind him, and he turned just as a crack of thunder resounded. The pitter-pat of rain sifted through broken glass and floorboards as did the creaking of wood from above. Owen tried to still his heart, breathing softly and straining to hear.

Muffled voices sounded overhead as something thumped on the floor. "What do you think made that hole?" a high-pitched voice said.

"I don't know," another whined. "The thing sure looks deep."

"Notice anything funny?" High Pitch said.

"You mean the sign that says Slow Children? I don't think it's funny. I think it's cruel. Those children can't help it that they're slow."

"No, I mean strange, like a noise that should be here but isn't."

A pause. "Like screaming and wailing and crying, people in pain, writhing, screeching, and bawling like animals that have just been stuck with a—"

"Would you please stop?"

"I was just telling you what I didn't hear," Whiner said.

"The buzzing. You know, from the minions."

"Oh. That. Yeah, I don't hear it either. What do you think happened to them? Could they be resting? All that buzzing must make them tired. Don't you think?"

Another pause. "How you were chosen to be a revellor for the Dragon, I'll never understand."

Revellor? Watcher had once described them as powerful,

ferocious, quick-as-lightning beings with sharp claws. Owen remained still. The voices didn't sound ferocious, but voices could be deceiving. He wanted to slip out the window and run, but he couldn't help wondering what they were doing here. What were they looking for? Minions?

Wings flapped and a third voice joined the other two, this one deep and sonorous (which means it boomed like the guy who announces the movie trailers at the theater). "What have you found?"

Whiner and High Pitch fought to answer, but Movie Voice stopped them. "Are you saying the minions are gone?"

"We don't hear them any longer," High Pitch said. "They could be underground, I suppose, waiting for daylight. . . ."

"Or they could be playing," Whiner said. "You know, like hide-and-seek. Only it would be hide-and-bite."

"Be quiet," Movie Voice said. "I've seen movement in the homes in the area. Not everyone has been stung. Not even close. If the minions are gone—"

"Maybe they made a mistake and moved to another town," High Pitch said.

"They do not make mistakes. They were sent here to find the Son and the two girls. To sting them all and make them of no use to the enemy."

"Maybe they did," Whiner said.

"Or perhaps the Son discovered some way to chase them

away." Movie Voice groaned. "At any rate, it is safe now. We can go back to His Majesty and report our findings."

"And the purging will begin?" Whiner said. "I can't wait."

Purging?

"Yes," Movie Voice said. "It is time to unite the worlds to honor the true king. And the people of this world must die."

3
The Sentence

Concerning the scruffy woman
who stands before the Dragon,
we must pause. We have glimpsed her
before in this castle, sleeping as her
husband kissed her. He then crept into
the shadows to leave the Lowlands,
but she remained. We have seen her
inside the mines with other workers.
We have even seen the interchange
between her and her Son, though she
did not know at the time that Owen
was her Son. *The* Son.

She had spoken harshly to the
Wormling and had regretted it. In
her misery she had told him she didn't
care about the uniting of the worlds,
that she only wanted her Son back.

A thousand times she wished she could have explained her reaction to someone in the mines. But when you are a queen, when you have been used to speaking with only a few trusted people, fearful that the enemy will send spies to ferret out information, you must keep quiet. But, oh, how her heart ached for her Son, her husband, her daughter, the entire Lowlands, and those in the Highlands as well—they had no idea what evil was coming. And now, here she stood, in a room that had once comforted her, among the enemies of her soul.

The brutes clapped and cheered in fake admiration as the Dragon smirked. Though her clothes weren't more than rags and she would have preferred being thrown into a pond of hungry alligators, she lifted her gaze to stare at the beings. One by one, as her eyes passed over the crowd, they seemed to lose their gusto.

The Dragon quickly backed to his throne and sat, waving for quiet. "Please, let us bestow a modicum of respect to this poor, beleaguered woman. After all, her husband is dead and we will soon hear of the demise of her Son as well."

The Queen narrowed her eyes at the Dragon.

"Her kingdom is in shambles, her friends and companions dead, and the one ray of hope, the Wormling, is but burnt toast on the ash heap of history. She is utterly alone."

If this was meant to evoke pity from this motley crew, it failed. They gloated all the more.

Finally the Dragon waved again. "My lady, you may think us uncaring and rude, but I remind you that we have every right as victors to drag your body through the streets in front of your subjects. But we did not do that, did we?"

The Queen continued to stare mutely at him.

"No, we did not," the Dragon said. "And I have good news for you. I am going to give you a chance to live."

The council members gasped.

"No, you must incinerate her now," General Prufro said.

"Show her your power," another chimed in.

The Dragon simply raised a lip, revealing a long incisor, and it silenced them. "No, a ruler can show power in many ways, and one is to present an alternative to annihilation. If you do as I say, I will not only let you live but will also allow you to take up residence here again."

Another gasp from the council.

"But, sire—," RHM said.

This time a snarl silenced him.

"What do you require?" the Queen said.

The Dragon stepped from his throne and settled on his belly on the floor, arms crossed under his chin, his face inches from the Queen's. His breath, a putrid mixture of charcoal and bad cheese, turned her empty stomach.

"Once the repairs have been made, I want you to accompany me to the coliseum and declare your allegiance, recognize your sovereign, bow your knee to me, and be allowed to live." The Dragon batted his eyelashes at the Queen in anticipation of her response.

With a fierceness that caused even those at the table to recoil, she spat, "My husband is the true King, and I shall never betray him, even at the cost of my life. He is the one with true greatness and glory and dignity and grandeur. You will never compare to him, and I could never bow my knee to you anywhere."

Except for a rattle deep in the Dragon's throat, there was no sound.

The Queen locked eyes with him. "And I still believe that the King's words will come true. The four portals shall be breached. The Son will return, and you will be defeated. And he will marry his bride."

"I could dispatch you with flames this very instant, woman," the Dragon said with an awful laugh. "Your Son is either already dead or so aged he wouldn't even be able to stand and say his vows. And your husband was dispatched long ago."

The Queen noticed RHM flinch and assumed he desired to correct his master. "Nothing you can say or do will make me worship you," she said. "Do with me as you wish, but do not waste your time or mine by threatening me."

The Dragon looked mad enough to incinerate the entire

castle, but instead he moved past the Queen to a painting on the wall that depicted the whole of the Lowlands. "This was one of your husband's favorites while he lived here. Notice particularly this part near the forbidden forests. Do you know what is there?"

The Queen peered at the painting, then looked away as council members chuckled and whispered.

"Yes," the Dragon purred. "A fate worse than death. Either you bow before me or I will send you to a place from which you will never return. Every day of your miserable life will be spent in agony at refusing my offer."

Sweat beaded on the Queen's brow, but with her hands tied she could not wipe it away. With quavering voice, she said, "I will never worship you."

The Dragon drew to within inches of her face again, and it seemed the very walls could crumble from the force of his voice. "I swear to make you regret those words! In front of these witnesses, you have committed high treason against your sovereign. You shall be banished from our midst and sentenced to live the remainder of your pathetic life among the outcasts of Perolys Gulch!"

The Queen lowered her head and shuddered. He was right. A fate worse than death.

4

The Noise

Of all the choices Owen had made
since learning he was the Son,
the most difficult was whether to slip
out the basement window and escape
this spooky place or stand and fight the
beasts above. He had read time and
again in *The Book of the King* that fear
would render him small.

Instead of running or brandish-
ing his weapon against three beings
who could slice and dice and make
french fries of him, Owen unsheathed
his sword and held it in front of his
mouth. "Zzzzzz," he said, tongue close
to the blade. The sound split, making
a metallic buzz much like that of the
minions of time.

Whiner said, "The minions are back. Let's get out of here before we get bitten ourselves."

Wings flapped and a gust of wind spurted through the keyhole.

Owen held his breath and waited, then buzzed louder, waving the sword. Water dripped through the charred building, and the floorboards creaked above. He leaned down to the keyhole and saw the hulking form of a huge revellor peering back at him. Owen jumped back, his heart beating wildly.

The doorknob turned and caught. The revellor spurted liquid through the keyhole, and as it hit the floor, it sizzled and bubbled and smoked like grease in a skillet. The metal doorknob was melting before his eyes.

Owen sheathed his sword and secured his pack, then wedged a rickety chair against the door. He rushed to the window, boards groaning under his feet, and crawled outside through the sharp glass. One of the shards cut him, but he kept going.

Once he had crawled out, he felt a lot better than being in the room with the creature, now banging and pushing on the door. Owen made it to the street, and rain soaked his hair and clothes. A flash of lightning illuminated the remnants of the building and a figure in the empty doorway. The being howled an unearthly cry that cut through Owen like a knife.

Owen raced into an alley much like the one he had run

through before he had discovered *The Book of the King.*
"Nicodemus," he said, gasping, "if you're near, I need your
help!"

Downspouts poured from surrounding roofs.

Should he have stayed to fight? Would the revellors
fly back to the Dragon and hasten the destruction of the
Highlanders?

Owen shook the water from his hair like a dog and tried to
think. *The Book of the King* instructed him to be courageous,
to fight his battles one by one, and to not despair, no matter
what the outcome. *The footsteps of the righteous are ordered by
the King. Though you may slip and fall, he will help you get back
on your feet.*

A wing flapped overhead, and a pang of fear shot through
Owen. He ducked into a stairwell and shivered, backing up as
far as he could into a brick wall, where he was sheltered from
the rain. He was trying to gather his wits when he felt a presence and heard a familiar voice.

"They will sense I am here," Nicodemus whispered, "and
they will know you are here as well."

"I need to find a place to hide and collect myself," Owen
said.

Though Owen could not see him, he imagined Nicodemus's
face, scrunched in thought, working out the problem.

"A woman you know lives nearby," Nicodemus said. "She

was your teacher—the one who was sent away." He gave
Owen the address and directions. "Now I must go."

"Wait," Owen said. "Did I do the right thing? Should I have
stayed to fight the beasts?"

Owen felt a hand on his shoulder. "Your heart is good,
young prince. There will come a time to fight, but for now it
is best to elude the enemy. Now go with haste. The darkness
may provide you with covering."

5

Mrs. Rothem

Owen stood at the end of a dark-ened hallway, his sword behind him, water dripping from his clothes and hair. The narrow hall left little room for him to hide, but he had found apartment 4D after jimmying the front door. It was still dark outside, which was eerie because the sunlight should have begun to invade.

He listened to a radio through the thin walls of 4C as well as the sounds of rattling pots and pans. His stom-ach clenched when he smelled bacon sizzling and imagined a skillet full of eggs, toast popping up, pancakes and syrup. . . .

Owen heard a news report about local authorities being baffled over reported attacks by bees "that people are saying don't look much like bees. The attacks began two days ago, and residents are warned to keep windows and doors shut and taped. Some believe this is simply a bad locust invasion, but many injured in the attacks are in serious condition at local hospitals."

Owen tapped lightly on 4D. A dull light shone under the door, but he saw no movement.

When he tapped again, the radio went silent and a door opened behind him. A chain tightened and an old, gray-headed woman peeked out of 4C and said, "What are you doing here? I'll call the police if you don't get out."

That was the last thing Owen needed. "I'm one of Mrs. Rothem's students," he said quickly. "Does she still live here?"

"Students don't come around here," the woman said. "How'd you get in? And how did you escape all those flying things?"

Owen kicked 4D with his heel.

"I'm calling the police," the woman said.

Just then, the door behind Owen opened and a shocked Mrs. Rothem stood there, her face contorted. "Owen? What are you doing here?"

"You know him?" the woman across the hall said.

"He's one of my best students. Come in. Come in."

It was a small apartment, with just a couch in the living room surrounded by makeshift bookshelves of milk cartons, wood, and cinder blocks. The kitchen table was small and had only two chairs. A single door led to a bedroom, where a nightstand was filled with books.

Owen moved to the window. "I'm sorry to bother you, Mrs. Rothem, but I needed a place to hide for a moment. Do you mind if I close these blinds?"

"Go ahead. What's wrong?"

"Surely you've heard of the creatures out there."

"Of course, but you've been gone so long. Where have you been?"

"It's hard to explain," he said, taking off his backpack.

"I read Clara's story in the school newspaper after I was transferred. We've all been quite concerned."

How much could Owen tell this woman?

"Let me get you some breakfast," she said. "Would you like that?"

"Very much."

"And hang your jacket in the bathroom. You can dry your hair in there."

Owen carefully placed his sword and jacket on the bathroom floor so as not to frighten Mrs. Rothem.

He returned to a cup of steaming tea, followed by a bowl of oatmeal, toast, and scrambled eggs. He ate hungrily as Mrs.

Rothem sat sipping her own tea. She put a pot of water on the stove, saying she would make lunch for him as well.

Mrs. Rothem crossed her arms. "You can trust me, you know."

Owen nodded and pulled *The Book of the King* out of his backpack. "A man gave me this. It changed my life."

She smiled as she took the book and ran her hands across the creases and rough spots. "Many lives have been changed through books."

"But it took me to a place that has no books," Owen said. "The people there are wonderful, but they aren't free. They are terrified of their enemy."

"And how did you get to this other world?" Mrs. Rothem said, leaning forward, eyes fixed on Owen.

He told her of Watcher and Mordecai and Nicodemus and the Scribe. He explained that the man who had given him the book was his real father, the flying minions who had come to the Highlands were from the Dragon, and his future and the future of the two worlds were intertwined.

Mrs. Rothem listened intently and gently leafed through the book, asking about his trip and what Owen had learned. He told her tame stories of the battles, but she didn't seem squeamish.

"Why do you suppose the Dragon lured you to the castle with this fake son?" she said.

"He knew the real Son wasn't there, but he wanted to trap me. Perhaps kill me. I'm the real Son."

"Does the Dragon know that?" Mrs. Rothem said. "Doesn't he think the Wormling and the Son are two people, just as you did?"

Owen paused. "He's the one who kidnapped me and brought me to the Highlands. Surely he knows."

She shook her head. "This may be why he sent these stinging animals—what did you call them?"

"Minions of time."

"If what you say is correct," Mrs. Rothem said, "Mr. Reeder may have covered for you. He may have told these beings that you slipped away and went into hiding—or that you were searching for the Wormling."

"It seems a stretch—"

"But it fits," she said, lowering her voice to a whisper.

Owen let the news sink in. If the Dragon still believed, as Owen had, that the Wormling and the Son were two people, he would have a better chance at defeating the old beast.

She looked deep in thought. "I spoke with the principal after I was transferred. She said your father—Mr. Reeder— was quite agitated about your being gone. But she did not doubt that he loved you."

He saw a twinkle in Mrs. Rothem's eyes, and she reminded him of the Queen back in the Lowlands.

She placed a wrinkled hand over his. "I always knew there was something special about you, Owen. I could see it in your eyes. I sensed it with every paper you wrote. To know you are royalty is a surprise, but I cannot think of a more deserving person—"

Suddenly shattering glass blew into the room as a hideous flying beast crashed to the floor.

Evil eyes seemed to study the two
at the table, wings twitching,
tentacles dripping a green liquid that
burned a hole in the floor.

A deep voice, the one Owen had
heard earlier talking to the other two
revellors, broke the silence. "So, your
secret is no longer a secret," the being
growled. "And the Dragon's questions
will be answered when I bring your
body to him. I'll receive a double
reward. Don't you think?" The beast
struggled to its feet but could barely
stand without hitting its head on the
ceiling.

Unless Owen could get back to the
bathroom, he was unarmed, except for

the book. He took it from Mrs. Rothem. "Stay still," he said, stepping between her and the beast. "Hear the words of the King!"

"I will listen to nothing from a defeated foe," the being said, shooting a stream at Owen's head.

Owen used the book to deflect the stream toward the kitchen, where it melted a hole in the window. The book was undisturbed. "'Though the forces of evil conspire against me, the sovereign plan of the King will—'"

"Do you think your empty words will defeat *me*?" the beast said, lips twitching and eyes red. "His Majesty, the Dragon, says this to your lifeless King." The monster rushed Owen and sent a blast of acidy poison from his mouth that reminded Owen of the demon vipers he had faced in the Lowlands. From its two biggest tentacles came two smaller blasts.

"Get down!" Owen yelled at Mrs. Rothem. He blocked the biggest stream but had to hurtle across the room to send the liquid behind him, creating a circle on the wall that sizzled and smoked, then crumbled in upon itself, revealing the bathroom.

The revellor pounced, but just as its razor-sharp jaws were upon Owen, he shoved *The Book of the King* inside its mouth and pushed with all his might, eluding the tentacles but barely budging the beast. With its wings spread behind it, the revellor caught itself in midair and dived at Owen, who sprang back into the hole in the wall. As plaster exploded around him, Owen rolled through pipes and over tile, plopping into the bathtub just as another stream of green goo struck the tub, ran to the bottom, and created a huge hole in the floor.

"What in the world . . . ?" a man said from his bathroom below.

"Sorry," Owen said. "Won't be much longer."

"Yes, not much longer," the revellor screeched, lunging at Owen.

As his enemy went airborne, Owen called for his sword and fell through the opening in the floor, landing beside the man, who stood there with a razor poised before his lathered face. Owen darted to the bathroom door and into the kitchen as something skittered and fell behind him.

A woman in curlers sat at the table, mouth full of pancakes, eyes wide as Owen barreled through with his sword. "Pardon me, ma'am, but I need to use your front door."

A horrible thump came from the bathroom. The man shouted, and then the woman screamed.

"Over here, Your Sliminess," Owen called. He closed the door behind him and took the stairs two at a time. He had made it to only the sixth step when the apartment door splintered and the revellor flew into the hall, scanning with giant insectlike eyes.

31

Owen held up the sword to block the next volley of liquid. The weapon glowed and created a protective shield around him, though it did not protect the nearby walls and doors.

The revellor blocked Owen's run for the next floor, so Owen changed direction. When someone opened an apartment door to see what was happening, the enemy was distracted and Owen headed back upstairs.

"Stay inside!" Owen hollered, fending off another spray.

When he reached Mrs. Rothem's floor again, he turned and met his enemy, using his sword to splatter the liquid back on the beast.

However, instead of weakening the monster, the stuff seemed to give it strength. "Now you will feel the wrath of the true king!"

Owen ran to the next flight of stairs, blocking more liquid and wondering whether the monster would ever run out.

Owen reached the top landing but found the door to the roof locked. The revellor hovered in the stairwell, and Owen could see down all five flights of stairs to the bottom.

"Ready to die?" the beast said.

"Actually, no," Owen said. Recalling from *The Book of the King*, he said, "'Your foot will not slip in your efforts for justice.'" He jumped onto the railing.

As the revellor flew at him, Owen dodged to his right, lopping off a tentacle that spiraled to the landing. With a screech, the monster nearly caught Owen with a slicing blow, but Owen blocked it and chopped off another tentacle with a quick jab.

Seething now and spitting blood, the revellor extended its wings to full width and swooped down on Owen.

He ducked just in time, but the force of the wind from the wings pushed him over the edge and into thin air. With nothing to break his fall, no arm in the night to catch him, at the last second Owen stuck his sword into the wood below the railing. Hanging by one hand, he saw the revellor rise in the air behind him like an eerie bird of prey, a smile on its blood-spattered lips.

Owen thought of his friends in the Lowlands. He thought of Clara and Mr. Page. What would they do when they discovered he had been killed by this fiend?

"You look pretty beat up, you venom-spitting piece of trash," Owen said. "Think you'll have enough energy to fly me back to Cinder-breath?"

"The Dragon will see these wounds as evidence of my devotion," the revellor said, rearing back for its final salvo. "Now you will die!"

Owen saw a figure on the landing just below move into the light. Mrs. Rothem held a huge, steaming pot with oven-mitted hands and, with a mighty heave, tossed boiling water onto the back of the flying beast.

The eyes of the revellor were full of hatred and envy until the scalding water hit its wings. They simply became of no use, so instead of shooting any more death poison at Owen, the beast fell straight back with a flurry and a skittering grab at anything on the way down.

Owen gained leverage with his feet and, with one hand grasping a slat of the stairway, pulled the sword out and threw it straight and true after the falling revellor. The sword ran through its heart and pinned it to the floor five stories below.

Owen jumped over the rail and dropped to Mrs. Rothem. "I knew you were a good English teacher, but I didn't know you could toss a bucket like that."

"English teachers are amazing," Mrs. Rothem said, staring below.

Owen called for his sword, then cleaned it on a towel in Mrs. Rothem's apartment.

She smiled. "I'm glad you came to see me."

"If all goes well, we'll see each other again."

As Owen was preparing to leave, Mrs. Rothem said, "I believe your task entails much more than simply reading and following this book."

Owen sheathed his sword. "Go on."

"When you read in my class, you often became so engrossed that you didn't even know when the bell rang. You lost yourself in the stories. But now you must do more. You must give of yourself to *his* story."

Owen nodded. "But there are things I don't understand. A girl is betrothed to me, yet I've never even dated anyone. And I'm not sure I can win the war with the Dragon."

Mrs. Rothem gave Owen the book and a look. "You will become more than a reader. Your life is bigger even than the enemies aligned against you and your father."

"Thank you," Owen said. He rushed downstairs, past the smoking, hissing hole in the floor and into the cloud-scattered day, where the sun had not yet begun to shine.

7
Kweedrum and Lambachi

RHM, the Dragon's aide, met with the two excited revellors—Kweedrum and Lambachi—near the Castle of the Pines. They had returned without their leader, Zeehof, after having been sent to see if the minions of time were succeeding. These two were—how shall we say this kindly?—not the best-tuned instruments in the orchestra.

RHM tried to pry information from them like an angry father pries a stolen cookie from a child.

Kweedrum pressed a talon into the sand as if drawing something. In a high-pitched voice he said, "We were reporting our discovery to Zeehof when the noise started again."

"What did he say?"

"He said a lot of things in that deep voice of his," Kweedrum said. "He mentioned that there was a 'human quality' to the buzzing of the minions, which was strange now that I think about it."

"Yes," Lambachi said, "it was very strange at the time, even, because we were all standing there ready to get stung or eaten or whatever those minions do to you, and then—"

"Okay, so we've established that it was strange," RHM snapped.

"We knew it would be the end of us if those minions started attacking, so we flew away."

"And Zeehof?" RHM said.

Lambachi coughed, then spoke with a whine. "He didn't follow us, and after the longest time we went back to look for him."

"No sign of him?"

"No, sir. But there was a smell of human in that room."

"Why didn't you stay until you found him?"

"We really didn't know what to do," Lambachi said. "We did wait awhile, but it was still dark and rainy and cold, and you know what that does to our wings. So we came back here as quickly as we could, knowing you would want a report."

RHM twitched at something cold moving up his back. It was the same feeling he'd had on the islands of Mirantha when he discovered the Wormling with his sword. "Did you check the nestor?"

"We didn't go any farther in the building once we heard the buzzing," Lambachi said.

"All right, listen carefully. Go back to the basement and find the nestor I placed there. When the minions have completed their task, they always return to the nestor."

"And then?" Kweedrum said.

RHM hesitated. "Uh, close the door and bring it back to me. And rest assured the Dragon will be particularly grateful for your work."

"A special reward?" Lambachi said, drooling.

"Oh yes. Quite."

8
Mr. Reeder

Owen cautiously made his way through town under the dark clouds. He passed old haunts, including his high school, which was closed tight and didn't look like it would ever reopen. He skirted the police station, wondering if Mr. Reeder might still be there. If he had been stung, which Owen had every reason to believe, they had probably taken him to the hospital.

Owen turned at a blinking red light and sprinted down a sidewalk covered with wet leaves. He wanted to make the most of every moment in the Highlands, and he had two stops before finding the final portal.

The emergency room was crowded, and an armed guard stood at the door. Owen pushed his scabbard behind him and pulled the hood of his jacket over his head.

The guard seemed perplexed by Owen's presence, as if surprised to see anyone outside. He opened the door wide enough only to pull Owen through. "What are you doing out there, man?"

"Looking for someone," Owen said, facing the man so he wouldn't notice the sword.

"Those biting things gone?"

"I think so," Owen said. "I hope so."

Owen listened to people calling out victims' names as he moved through the jammed hallways. People who had been stung sat propped against walls, moaning, some writhing. All looked aged and frail. Tears suddenly blurred Owen's vision. Several times he thought he saw Mr. Reeder, but he could tell by friends standing around that it wasn't. Mr. Reeder was a loner, and Owen could count his friends on one hand.

"Owen?" someone said from a dark hallway. "Owen Reeder? Is that you?" Staggering toward him was an old man, wrinkled and bowlegged, a little taller than Owen. Something about his eyes and the lilt of his voice reminded Owen of someone.

"Do I know you?" Owen said.

"Owen, it's me, Stanley. Stanley Drones." Stanley was a burly kid with broad shoulders and an interesting pattern of brown spots on his face. He still wore the long-billed cap—his trademark—but white hair stuck out from beneath it, and the peach fuzz on his face had grown out gray.

"You were stung," Owen said, unable to think of anything else to say.

"Master of the obvious," Stanley said, managing a weak smile. "And you weren't, but it sure looks like you've been working out. Where have you been?"

Owen pulled his friend back into the shadows to one of a few secluded doorways and unsheathed his sword.

"Did I say something wrong?" Stanley said.

"No, I have to try something."

"I don't suppose it could hurt," Stanley said. "I don't have much time left anyway."

"Where were you stung?"

Stanley pulled up his shirt and with a pained face pointed to his rear. "Sank his teeth in there and wouldn't let go. The look on the thing's face as he came in for the kill was awful. You should have heard it hissing and growling. Last time I wear those jeans that ride low."

Owen held the sword against Stanley's wrinkled skin, causing him to flinch, and Owen imagined the skin tightening and his hair turning brown. But no.

"The metal's kinda cold," Stanley said, teeth chattering. "What were you doing?"

"My sword has the power to restore," Owen said. "I thought it might work on you."

Stanley looked at Owen as if he had suddenly grown another head. "Power? I guess I shouldn't doubt anything these days. Where did you find this sword?"

"I'll fill you in when there's time. Have you seen my father?"

Stanley shook his head.

Owen nodded and patted his friend on the shoulder. "I'm sorry."

"Not half as sorry as we are. If they don't find some kind of serum for this, we're all going to die."

Owen had covered every floor and corridor when he came to the top story and a closed wing with a sign that read Terminal. From a room down the hall two men wheeled a sheet-covered body. Owen slipped inside and held the door open for them as they passed.

Old people sat or lay on the floor, looking uncomfortable, in fact near death. Owen peeked into rooms with only two beds but five or six people crowded inside. Emotion swept over him. They would all die unless someone could help them.

A hand touched his shoulder, and he turned quickly.

"I didn't mean to scare you," a woman said with a slight

accent. She was pretty and wore a green hospital gown. It was clear she hadn't been stung, but she also looked like she hadn't slept in a long time. "You shouldn't be back here. It's only for—"

"I'm looking for my father. His name is Reeder."

A look crossed her face. "Come with me."

At the end of the hall was a curtained area containing several cots. "Our most serious cases," the woman said. "Multiple stings." She raised her voice slightly. "Mr. Reeder?"

A woman turned on her side, and her cot creaked.

In the corner by a window with the shutter closed, a figure raised his head.

"Talk with him," the nurse said. "Maybe you can ease the pain of his last moments."

Mr. Reeder had not only grown much older, but he had also become more sallow, skin hanging from his bones. He reached out a bony hand and feebly patted the empty cot beside him.

Owen wanted to try his sword, but if it hadn't worked with Stanley, how could it work with Mr. Reeder? "I didn't mean to leave you alone in the police station, but the minions said they had found someone. I had to follow."

Mr. Reeder waved. "I should have gone too. But I was doomed."

"You have to fight," Owen said. "You must survive this."

Mr. Reeder wheezed, "There's not much I can do about it. The doctors don't understand the venom. They've given us no hope."

Owen searched the man's face in the dim light. "I need to ask you something. The things you told me at the police station about both worlds—where did you hear about that? From the Dragon's henchmen?"

"No. They told me of the Dragon, that he would attack if I didn't hold up my end of the bargain."

"Then who told you about the two worlds?"

Mr. Reeder's eyes glazed over and he lay back, sucking in air. "There was a visitor. A voice. He whispered about the Lowlands, about the King."

"Nicodemus," Owen said.

"I didn't get a name. And I didn't believe much of what he said. I thought I was going crazy."

"When I told you I had heard a voice, you got angry with me. You said, 'This is all there is.'"

"A battle raged in me over whether to believe those strangers in cloaks that I could see or the voice in the dark that I could not see."

"What else did he say?"

"He told me fantastic things, things I couldn't believe. That there was another world much like our own, but it was populated with people and beings who were the mirrors—"

"Mirrors?" Owen said. "Explain."

"I asked, but the voice didn't want to converse. He simply informed me."

"Tell me more. Tell me all of it."

Owen's mind reeled as Mr. Reeder talked. Faces of his friends in both worlds came to mind, and he wondered how much of this could be true. Things were coming together. Terrible things. Wonderful things. And he understood, at least partly, why he was so important to both worlds.

"What troubles you?" Mr. Reeder said, eyelids fluttering.

Owen leaned forward, his face in the light. "You must keep fighting. The voice was right. You do have a son. I have seen him. He's so full of life. And he is waiting for you."

"Tell me about him," Mr. Reeder said.

Owen described the blond-haired boy, and Mr. Reeder's eyes flashed with fire. "He is waiting for you, but you must survive this. If I am right, any hope you have of uniting with your family depends on your survival."

"But even the doctors have no idea how to counteract the venom!"

Owen thought a moment. "Are you prepared to do what it takes to survive?"

"Anything."

Owen carefully unsheathed his sword.

A woman gasped. "You're going to kill us."

"No," Owen said. "Keep quiet and watch." He pulled back Mr. Reeder's shirt, revealing pale skin draped over his rib cage. "I don't want to hurt you, but if you are to survive, I must."

Mr. Reeder flinched, eyeing the blade.

Owen said, "*The Book of the King* says, 'The King can heal the broken heart and bind the stings of the enemy.' But unless your wound is fresh, and you're willing, I can't do anything."

Mr. Reeder put his hand on Owen's arm. "I'm willing."

Owen placed the tip of the blade against the man's side, locking eyes with him, and pushed. Mr. Reeder's eyes widened.

"He's killing him!" the woman shouted.

Mr. Reeder's mouth popped open, lips trembling. "Quiet," he managed. "He's trying to help."

Owen pulled the blade out and wiped the blood on his pant leg, then examined the wound. Dark blood pooled thick and heavy near the cut. Owen wondered whether the venom somehow thickened the blood as it aged the victim.

"Why did you do that?" Mr. Reeder said, choking. "I don't see how piercing me will help me survive."

Owen pressed the blade over the wound, and in the dim light color seemed to come back to Mr. Reeder's face and his eyes went from filmy and dull to bright. His breathing became more even and he sat up, staring into Owen's eyes. "Could you do this for others?" he said.

"Not for those who don't want it or don't acknowledge their need."

Mr. Reeder nodded. "Where will you go?"

"I have one more person to see."

9

Request

It was still raining, and lightning pierced the sky. It took Owen an hour to find the right street and the building, but he finally buzzed the apartment. He stepped back and looked up at the window where he had once seen his friend Connie. The apartment she shared with her mother was dark, the curtains pulled.

He climbed the wet stones on the side of the building but found the windows fastened tight. He could tell no one was there.

When Owen heard a siren in the distance, he scrambled down, assuming someone had seen him and called the police. He ducked into the alley and hid near the trash cans.

The cruiser, however, did not stop.

"You will not find her here," someone said behind him.

Finally accustomed to whispers in the dark, Owen casually turned but saw no one. "Nicodemus? You followed me?"

"I am to ensure you make it to the portal."

"Where's Connie?"

"Not far. But I must warn you. There may be things still too difficult for you to understand."

"What things?"

"You know the identity of Mr. Reeder—that he is linked to a father in the other world."

"Yes, and I've been making the connections of friends. Stanley Drones, Petrov who works next door at the Blackstone Tavern, and even Mrs. Rothem."

"Good," Nicodemus said. "Everyone you know in this world has someone—or had someone—to whom they are connected in the other."

"Had?" Owen said. "You mean like Mr. Reeder's—the one I found frozen into the side of the mountain?"

"Yes."

"You talked with Mr. Reeder, Nicodemus. You told him about the family in the Lowlands. You convinced him there was more than this world."

"Yes. He had bought the Dragon's lies that only the things you can see are real. Whether from true belief or simply wishful thinking, he complied with our request."

"So there is hope for someone who has died in the Lowlands but still lives here," Owen said.

"Correct."

"And if both die?"

Nicodemus paused. "The death of the first leaves one choice. There is no hope for the second death."

"What about me?" Owen said. "Do I have a match somewhere in this world?"

"No. You need no match, Your Highness. You are the Son."

Owen sighed. "I have to find Connie."

Another pause. "Perhaps it would be better if I simply told you she is safe. You need to get to the portal and—"

"I have to talk with her," Owen said.

"Your presence may endanger the young lady," Nicodemus said. "You wouldn't want that."

"Please, I really need to talk with her and make sure she's all right."

"Very well," Nicodemus said. "But there is something you must see first."

10

Connie

Unless Connie looked in a mirror, she couldn't see the aging effects, except for on her hands, now wrinkled and spotted.

Equally frightening was the aging process of her mind. You might think she would have remained a girl in her brain, just a young thing trapped in an old thing's body, but no. The venom worked on every aspect of her being—her muscles, her heart, her brain. Even her memories were affected, clouded by time that had never been but was suddenly thrust upon her.

Clara waited on her, bringing her something to drink and making sure she was warm and as comfortable as an old, dying person can be. Connie could tell she was dying by the way Clara looked at her. Though she had suffered just one sting, the beast was oversized and had sunk its fangs in deep. Mr. Page had looked concerned when he had brought her here, as if her growing old was not the only thing that troubled him. What could it have been? Did he know something he wasn't telling?

"Mr. Page said I was to take you to a safe place as soon as you are well enough to travel," Clara said.

"With those things out there?" Connie said, her voice shaky.

"He said he would take care of them," Clara said. "How do you feel?"

"Like this is the last day I will spend on earth."

"You mustn't talk like that," Clara said, drawing closer. "You have a wonderful future."

"What? An hour? Perhaps a day?"

"Mr. Page says you are destined for greatness. Nothing can stop the King's plans."

"What are you talking about?" Connie said.

Clara drew close. "Mr. Page told me everything. He wrote it down and even gave instructions on how to care for you. Where to take you." She paused as if trying to figure out what to share and what to hold back. "You and I were both separated from our parents long ago. I lived in another world, a place of wonder and beauty and talking animals."

"Talking animals?"

"Yes. But I was brought here, along with my brother, and we were separated. We are children of the King, though we haven't known it."

"Well, that's great for you and your brother. You two should have enough money to bury me."

"You don't understand. Mr. Page told you long ago that you were destined to become a queen."

The effects of the venom had caused Connie to despair. She had always been filled with faith and hope, but now, with her life ebbing, she became bitter. "I don't remember anything."

Clara put a cool washcloth against her forehead. "Think," she whispered. "The boy you knew as Owen is becoming a man. He is the Son of the King. He is to be your husband."

"Owen?" she said. "Wasn't he here not long ago?"

"And he came to see you, knowing you would be his bride but not recognizing you as his old friend."

"Old is right."

Clara knelt before Connie and pushed a shock of gray hair from her forehead. "You have been chosen before you were even born to be *his* bride."

"Why me?" Connie said. "What would make me fit to be the wife of the Son of the King?"

Clara smiled. "Mr. Page said you have a purity of heart he has rarely seen. You are very special to him."

"Special and old," Connie said, chuckling ruefully.

"Do you think you can get up?" Clara said.

"I can try."

Kweedrum and Lambachi were
headed to the basement of the
B and B to find the nestor for RHM
when they spotted a glowing object
moving through the streets. Dazzled
by the light and frightened by the task
ahead, they soared above the treetops
until alighting on a roof across the
street from a great stone building.

"I wonder what that is," Lambachi
said.

"It looks like one of those places
where they keep all those things with
words in them," Kweedrum said.

"No, not the building. That light."

"It looks like a torch. And there's someone beside it. How can he be walking in the street with all the minions around?"

"Maybe he's protected by the glow."

The door mysteriously opened, and the glow moved inside, along with the other figure.

"Strange," Kweedrum said. "I don't know anyone who can do that, unless it's one of *his*."

"Stop referring to *him* or you'll bring down the wrath of His Majesty on us," Lambachi said. "But if you're right, if this is one of *his* messengers, that other figure might be the one His Majesty seeks."

"The nestor? I thought it was at that old building—"

"Not the nestor, you ninny."

"I'm not a ninny! Take it back."

"All right, you're not a ninny. I'm talking about the Wormling."

"No, the Wormling is dead," Kweedrum said. "Haven't you heard? His Majesty incinerated him inside the White Mountain."

"Then who could this be?"

"The Son. The last hope of the enemy. Can you imagine if we returned to RHM with him?" Kweedrum licked at his mouth. "They would throw a party. And maybe a parade— where everybody lines up and walks around with those fancy

clothes and people clap and cheer, and if they don't, the
Dragon blows fire at them."

"Perhaps more would happen. Perhaps we would be made
princes over a province."

"Princes over a province," Kweedrum repeated. "What
would that be like? I mean, what's the job description?"

"We would be like His Majesty. Rulers. People would bow
before us and obey our every command. We would have
mountains of food and true power."

"It sounds like a nice job. And you think all we have to do
is capture this Son person?"

"That and kill the messenger of light. We cannot let him
escape."

"Of course not. That would be awful. We should kill him
first because then the Son will be so scared he'll probably
cower under the tables or even surrender."

Lambachi drew up a plan, while Kweedrum nodded and
tapped his lips with the side of one wing, smiling and letting
a little spittle escape. "You should have been a general in His
Majesty's army," Kweedrum said. "You really have a knack for
attack."

Lambachi took the compliment and gushed. He had once
attempted to become a warrior, but his wings were too large
and bulky for all the marching and processions. He had been
chosen as a revellor for his ability to act sinister despite his

low intellect. "We'll catch them by surprise, kill the messenger, bind the human, and discover who he is. Then we'll retrieve the nestor and return to RHM with our prizes."

"And become princes of a province," Kweedrum said.

They glided down as quietly as they could, but the rain made it difficult. They landed with thumps and shook the rain from their backs like dogs. Except these dogs had sharpened talons and fangs that could rip the entrails out of a man with one swipe.

They peered into the stone building, locked in on their prey, and rose as one.

12
The Waters of Words

Owen followed the glowing robe of
Nicodemus (if you're wondering,
it was the first time Owen had ever
seen it glow) through the rain-battered
streets, sloshing in the standing water.
They were a curious pair to any who
cared to look out their windows,
though surely many did not care to,
fearing the stinging, flying beasts.

They stopped at one of the oldest
stone buildings in town, the library.
The front door was locked, but something clicked and it opened. Owen
looked at Nicodemus and began to ask
but decided to simply follow him.

The familiar smell of old books hit
Owen and brought back thoughts of

the used-book store and his countless hours of reading among the full shelves. He had thrown himself into those books just as he had thrown himself into the Lowlands and his battles. Like a child leaping from a riverbank and submerging himself in cool waters, Owen had jumped headfirst into the swirling stories that surrounded him, sometimes not coming up for air for days. At times he forgot to eat, so lost was he in the pages.

He had learned immeasurable things in the waters of words. He had enjoyed the classics, contemporary stories, and those in between. Fairy tales had been his favorite when he was younger. Later he moved to the Hardy Boys (and when no one was looking, even Nancy Drew), then to classics such as *A Christmas Carol* and *Charlotte's Web*. Owen loved *Where the Red Fern Grows*. He cried at the deaths of the dogs (we apologize if you have not yet read that book, but we have not told you which dogs) and moved on to other works. Owen even enjoyed reading old encyclopedias. He would read just about anything, and the smell of the books and the wooden shelves and floors made him want to take up residence here.

"Why are we going inside?" Owen said.

"There's a newspaper article you must see." Nicodemus led Owen to a computer and gave him a date to key in. The masthead of the local paper appeared.

"Go to the Metro section," Nicodemus said.

What Owen saw next took his breath. The headline read

"Missing Couple Believed Dead." A man and woman stood side by side, the woman holding a baby. Owen gaped. "It's the king and queen of the west."

"And what do you know about them?"

"They are the parents of the princess Onora, the one betrothed to me. But how . . . ?"

"The reason they are not the true king and queen is that they are not of the Lowlands. They are from the Highlands."

"Yes," Owen said. "I discovered that. What happened?"

"The Dragon transported them through the kingdom of the air. He took them to the Lowlands and made a treaty with them, promising to return them to their daughter at the appointed time, after the threat to his reign was over. Now he has violated that treaty and has vowed that Onora's blood will anoint his throne."

"But I met the princess in the shack, the one where Mr. Page—my father—was staying."

"Yes, that is Onora, though she has aged because of the minion's venom."

Owen's mind raced. The article said the two had disappeared along with their baby. "What happened to the child, to Onora, when her parents were taken away?"

"She came under the care of a lowly cleaning lady. Though she was married, because of the Dragon's requirements, she did not stay with her husband but cared for the child alone."

Owen started to ask more, but Nicodemus put a finger to his lips. "I can tell you no more about her."

"Then tell me about Onora," Owen said. "She has a match in the Lowlands?"

"Of course. It was the King's good pleasure all along to unite those in the Highlands with their counterparts in the Lowlands. This is part of your task. Do you remember the passage from *The Book of the King*?"

Owen searched his memory. "'Happy are those who have not seen the King and still believe what he has said. They shall be set free by knowing the truth and shall be partakers of the wholeness the world will soon see.'"

"Excellent," Nicodemus said. "Do you understand now?"

Owen stared at the flickering screen. "I'm to marry Onora, the old woman here, whose match . . ." He thought of all the people and beings he had met in the Lowlands. One face stayed with him. One friend who was closer than any family member he had ever had. He looked up. "Watcher?"

Nicodemus nodded solemnly.

"I can think of no one better to spend my life with than someone as faithful and trustworthy as Watcher," Owen said. "But marrying such an old person . . . and one who is part . . ."

"Were you going to say 'animal'? It is not the type of creature in the Lowlands that is important. It is the heart of the being." Nicodemus turned off the computer. "And she does not have to remain old. There is a way to restore her."

"How?" Owen said.

"That I cannot tell you. But she must survive her sting here, for . . ."

Owen looked at Nicodemus, but all he could see was the glowing robe. "What? What were you going to say?"

"I've said enough already," Nicodemus said. "You will discover the rest in time."

"The rest?"

"The Highland identity of Onora."

Owen had come to understand that only part of the puzzle would be unveiled to him at a time. "But I don't understand. I know you said the Son has no match, but if everyone has a mirror in both worlds, why not the Son?"

Nicodemus chuckled. "The one who brings wholeness must himself be whole. There is no other part to you, Owen. There is nothing more that can be added to your good heart. You are complete because you are the Son of the King."

"Then that means my sister, Clara—or what is she called in the Lowlands?"

"Gwenolyn," Nicodemus said.

"So is Gwenolyn complete in herself as well?"

"No, she has a reflection in the Lowlands also."

"If she was taken when we were young, wouldn't the reflection or other person be here?"

Nicodemus turned. "Your question is presumptuous."

Owen had heard the word before. *Presumptuous* meant he had made a faulty assumption, had presumed something. He had thought something about the King that wasn't true. But what?

"You assume the King lacks power."

"I do no such thing. It is simply that when a person is here, there is a reflection in the other realm. It is his way."

"Yes, but you do not give the King credit. He knew before it would even happen that Gwenolyn would be taken. And that you would be as well."

"So he placed her *other part*—or whatever you call it—in the Lowlands?"

"Precisely."

"Wait," Owen said. "If he knew we would be taken, he knew about Mordecai. He knew Bardig would die at the hands of Dreadwart. He knew what I would endure."

"Yes, and he believed it worth the discovery. And love."

"Love?"

"A subject of the King who is forced to act does not do so out of love but compulsion. He or she is obligated to comply. But one who acts of his own free will out of a sense of gratitude and honor is the person who truly loves. Who truly follows."

"What about you, Nicodemus? Do you have an equal in some other world?"

"I am simply a messenger of the King. I was given one chance to choose to either follow the true King or his enemy." Owen was about to ask the fate of the King, his father, but the crashing of glass behind him sent him to the ground as two unearthly beings flew into the library and dived for the kill.

13

Nicodemus

Glass flew everywhere as Owen
threw up his hands and ducked.
Nicodemus pushed him hard behind
the circulation desk, a wooden monstrosity near the front. Owen fell in a
heap as glass tinkled around him and
something wild screeched above. He
looked back just in time to see a suddenly visible Nicodemus trying to fend
off the swooping attackers.

Nicodemus flew backward, tumbling
over the computers and catapulting
into the first row of stacks, knocking
the shelves into each other like domi-
noes and sending them to the floor.
Books flew everywhere as Nicodemus
crashed to the floor.

Owen froze when the revellors shot past him and hovered over Nicodemus, their enormous wings showering water droplets throughout the room. They were much like the one he had faced at Mrs. Rothem's building, though these two looked scrawnier and didn't have quite the same evil aura. However, when they shot sizzling saliva at Nicodemus, Owen could tell they were out for blood.

No matter how comical a foe looks at a glance, the truth is that if they have sworn their allegiance to the enemy, we must not laugh at them or do anything but pity their foolish choices.

Owen could have stayed hidden or even crawled away, but as we have said, when the heart of a lion beats inside the chest of what otherwise looks like an average young man, he cannot help but spring forth in heroic fashion.

Owen leaped to his feet and brandished the Sword of the Wormling.

Four eyes flashed fire, and the winged creatures abandoned the motionless Nicodemus and shot their venom toward Owen.

He deftly avoided the streams and jumped to his right, a stack of books breaking his fall and propelling him. He dodged another volley of acid and retreated (or so the beasts had to believe) behind a large metal bookcase.

"You take that side. I'll take this," one said with a hiss. Owen understood because of his sword.

"But what about the nestor?" the other said. "I could let you take care of this while I go—"

"Forget the nestor for now and concentrate! That must be the Sword of the Wormling."

Catlike, Owen climbed the shelves and perched on top as the slower revellor peeked around the side. Owen jumped, his sword in front of him, and plunged it deep into the back of the creature. A geyser spurted and there came a screech so demonic and otherworldly that Owen nearly covered his ears. Had he done so, he wouldn't have had time to extract the sword and plunge it into the belly of the second beast that flew from the other end of the bookshelf and nearly devoured him. But that final thrust into the heart of the revellor killed it instantly, and Owen fell back, the beast's long neck and left wing covering him.

Owen struggled to escape from between the heavy creatures without the liquid scorching him. The one below made a final, desperate lunge at Owen, but he drove the sword into the top of the creature's head and down through its mouth until it finally stopped squirming. Venom seeped from the wounds and consumed the bodies as they shrank, hissing, into the wooden floor.

Owen ran to Nicodemus, whose robe no longer glowed.

Owen clawed at the books strewn over his body and pushed them away. His old friend and protector stared straight ahead, eyes fixed.

"Nicodemus," Owen whispered, lifting him, "don't leave me. I need you."

Though Nicodemus's lips didn't move, Owen heard him clearly. "You haven't needed me since the moment I met you."

"I needed you the night I almost fell into that hole in the street."

A smile appeared on the being's face. "You have come a long way since that night. You are strong, Owen. But your strength comes from inside. From your heart."

Owen pulled out his sword and placed it against Nicodemus's chest, but nothing happened. "I thought you would live forever."

"Only one is eternal, and all life springs from him."

"What has become of my father? Will I ever see him again?"

Nicodemus struggled. "You are not alone, young prince. Keep the book close until every word is fulfilled. And remember what I have said. No matter what you find—or what finds you."

"Remember?" Owen said, leaning close, straining to hear. "Remember what?"

Nicodemus lay back, and his words were as faint as a passing breeze. "The enemy will know when those two don't return. Make haste. Fulfill your destiny."

"They spoke of a nestor," Owen said. "Do you know what that is?"

"Queen of the minions," Nicodemus said, choking. "Very dangerous. It is death to you but also a weapon. . . ."

"Please," Owen said. "Don't leave."

"'No good thing is ever easy,'" Nicodemus whispered. And then he faded from Owen's sight, leaving only books where he had lain.

14

Love Note

His heart breaking, Owen ran
through the murky half-light
of day and made his way back to the
shack where he had left Clara and the
old woman.

When last they had talked, the old
woman had seemed to know him. And
something in her eyes reminded him of
someone he had met before—but who?

A passage from *The Book of the King*
flashed through his mind. The point
was that if you truly wanted to hide
something from someone, you should
put it right in front of them until it
became so familiar they didn't see it
for what it really is.

Perhaps that was the plan of the

enemy in regards to Owen's bride. Perhaps the very thing he would treasure, had he known her true identity, was a person who seemed to him a nuisance, and the drum of her life had beaten in the background until it became so common that he didn't hear it any longer.

Owen found the shack dark, not even a candle burning inside, and the place was still. "Clara?" he whispered.

A chill ran up Owen's back. He had been in enough of these situations to know that silence was not good. He peeked inside the bedroom. Was someone in the bed? Would the Dragon jump out at him?

He pulled the covers back to reveal a couple of old pillows. A piece of paper fluttered to the floor. He remade the bed, making sure it was lumpy like before, and took the paper back to the front room. In the muted light coming through the window he read:

> *Owen,*
> *Clara is writing for me, as I have very little strength left. By now you know who I am and what the future holds. I can't imagine you would want to marry a little chattering girl like me—who has become an old chattering woman. Perhaps there is some mistake, but Clara says your father does not make mistakes and that we should trust his plan. I don't understand much of this, but I do know that you are without equal—in this world and whatever other world is out there. I don't know the future, but I do know who*

holds it, and I believe he will help you achieve the ends he has purposed for you.

I knew from the moment I met you that you were special. Little did I know how special.

I cannot say more, except that Clara is taking me to a safe place where I will be able to rest and recuperate. Perhaps it will help me become young again so that you will not look at me with pity but with hope and love.

I will wait for you, Owen Reeder. I will wait for the Son. And I will pray that your father's strength will bring you back to me. I can't wait to see you again.

With all my love,
Connie

Owen fell, his knees hitting the floor with a thud. He read the note again and again, then folded it carefully and put it in his pocket. Out in the woods the fog was lifting, as if some unseen hand were preparing a way through the chilly morning.

"Connie," he whispered. "Onora. I will find you. Hold on until I do."

15
The Bargain

RHM flitted nervously about the castle meeting room, variously rearranging chairs, biting the ends of his talons and spitting them in the corner, and staring out the window. Though the Dragon seemed quite happy with himself and the progress in the Lowlands, RHM knew one bad report could bring the wrath of the old beast down on him.

Unfortunately for RHM, the return of Slugspike and a gaggle of his hangers-on coincided with the Dragon's descent down the wide spiral staircase. The Dragon had spent the night eating and drinking and blowing fire so that people even miles from the castle could see flames shooting from the upstairs windows. Anyone close enough could hear the screams of the victims as well.

RHM had fretted all through the night and into the morning waiting for news from Slugspike, and now that he had returned, the Dragon just *happened* to waltz downstairs.

"And where have you been, my overgrown friend?" the Dragon said to Slugspike. "You should have been here for the revelry last night."

Slugspike glanced at RHM as if to say, "He didn't know where I was?"

RHM responded with a smirk that could not be translated.

Slugspike bowed low. "I was on an errand for you, O great one, in the Highlands—"

"Yes, we wanted to surprise you with the good news," RHM interrupted from behind. "It *is* good news, is it not?"

"If the absence of minions is good news," Slugspike groaned. He was such an evil presence that the general reaction of everyone was to back away. "We found evidence of their demise and also evidence of the havoc they wreaked."

"Demise?" the Dragon said.

"A hole in the earth near the resting place of the nestor. The cage was empty. It looked like it had escaped from inside and led the whole company down after something."

"Then we have nothing to fear from them," the Dragon said with a smile. "We can attack the survivors or bring them here."

"Yes, Your Majesty," Slugspike said. He gave RHM another glance. "But I must report a slightly disappointing situation."

The Dragon was idly picking through scorched food on the table, apparently unconcerned. "Yes, go on."

"We have searched for the girl Onora as well as Gwenolyn. We cannot find them or the boy who had the device inserted in his heel."

"That was cut out and tossed away long ago," the Dragon said, grinding his teeth. "Perhaps they were stung and have crawled off into some hovel to die. They could be dead already."

"True, sire," Slugspike said. "However, we have located the ones charged with watching those two and have brought them."

"Really? Here?" the Dragon said, rising to peer out the window.

RHM sidled close and sneered at the sight of the humans. One was tall with a long nose and white hair. His name in the Highlands was Mr. Reeder. The other was a squat woman with equally white hair who looked to be in pain.

"What of the two who were watching Gwenolyn?" RHM said. "I gave you specific instructions to—"

Slugspike gave RHM a look that stopped him, as if all the motivation he needed to kill RHM was to hear one more word. "Those two were sputtering some gibberish, out of their minds from their stings, advancing in age by the second. We put them out of their misery."

"Bring the live ones to me," the Dragon said.

♦♦♦

Mr. Reeder trembled at the sight of the Dragon and stared at the floor. Mrs. Reeder (who had simply been known to Owen as the woman who cleaned up after them and Connie's mother) could not even stand in the Dragon's sight and fainted. Mr. Reeder knelt to tend to her.

The Dragon sniffed at the two like a dog who smells another animal on a person's clothes. He dribbled green liquid on them but finally backed away and gazed at Mr. Reeder. "What has become of the boy put in your charge?"

Mr. Reeder's chin quivered, and his legs, thin as matchsticks, knocked against each other like a metronome in a hurricane. With a stammer he managed, "He left the bookstore."

"When?"

"Shortly after the strange man showed up. I tried to keep the man from him, but—"

"And who do you think that man was?" the Dragon said.

"Just a beggar. He wore old clothes. He had an odd look in his eyes. But he also had a magical book with him that enchanted the boy."

"Where is he now?"

"I haven't seen the old man—"

"Not the man, the boy. His Son!"

"Son?" Mr. Reeder said. "That was the boy's real father?"

The Dragon snarled and looked at the woman, who began to awaken. "Would you like me to dispatch your wife now or wait until you tell me the truth?"

"I am telling the truth!" Mr. Reeder said, and had Owen been there, he would have been surprised at the man's passion and sudden bravado. "I tried my best to do everything I was told."

"But you allowed the boy to meet the Wormling!" the Dragon said.

"I did no such thing. He left the store only to go to school or on an errand. I swear it."

"He met this Wormling sometime after he discovered the book," the Dragon said. "That must be where he is now. Hiding. Waiting. Hoping."

"I know nothing of what you are saying."

"Really?" the Dragon said. And with a turn of his shoulder and an intake of breath so subtle the man barely heard it, the Dragon shot flame with great precision at Mr. Reeder's wife.

The woman barely whimpered before her life was over.

But we shall focus on Mr. Reeder's face, for there was something unnatural there—something we have not seen before. From the moment we first met him, he appeared a man mastered by other forces, who has allowed life to bully him. But as he looked at the charred remains of what was once a living, breathing woman with a load of fears and difficulties of her own, something changed.

Muscles tight, his teeth clenched, he turned to the enemy of the King and his Son. "All right. I'll tell you. But I want assurances."

"You are in no position to bargain, my friend," the Dragon said.

"You do not know what I know."

The Dragon stared at him as if admiring the man's backbone, especially after having just seen his wife struck down. "Very well. If you have solid information about the one I am after, I am in a position to make it worth your while."

"I have given up much to be loyal to you, and you repay me with the death of my wife. I want a place at your side. A place of prominence."

"You must have something juicy for me." The Dragon turned to RHM. "We have a place in the kingdom box at the coliseum, do we not?"

"Yes, sire, but—"

"If you give me truly helpful information," the Dragon said, "you will enjoy a seat where every spectator and combatant in the coliseum will see you. You will be envied."

"Then listen carefully," Mr. Reeder said, whispering in the Dragon's ear.

16

Buried Dreams

And now, though it pains us, we
visit the valley near the forest of
Emul, which in time shall be known
as the Valley of Death and later by
another name—for reasons you will
see. It is a peaceful place, with mounds
of dirt scattered across the hillside like
someone has been digging for hidden
treasure. It has the feel of a cemetery,
quiet and languid. Even the trees seem
to slow their swaying in the breeze.
Some have been blackened by the
heat of battle. A few have bloomed
and already returned to their original
beauty.

Above the trees, the sky is blue and
dotted with clouds rolling lazily past

as if unaware of what has gone on below. Of the grief that has gripped the countryside. Of the sorrow and tears and dreams that have been planted for harvest.

Something winged flits about, just under the tree branches. It is Batwing, the diminutive creature who has remained with the others to bury those who have been so mercilessly killed by the Dragon's forces.

Among the survivors are Rogers, the deep-voiced young-ster who had been a stable boy for the king of the west, and Starbuck, the son of Erol and a friend of the Wormling. Tusin, assemblyman of the undergroundlings, is also here.

"That is the end," Starbuck says. "The very last of them. Except for the horse. I don't think we can dig a hole large enough to—"

"Humphrey was his name," Rogers says. "Please don't refer to them without using their names. We should never forget their names or what they tried to do."

Starbuck turns. "You're not the only one who lost those you love."

"Young ones, don't quarrel," Tusin says. "We must hold together."

"For what purpose?" Starbuck says. "The Dragon has won. He's defeated us."

"As long as the King lives, there is hope," Tusin says. "Remember that and do not despair."

"My father, mother, brothers, and sisters are buried here. I should have been as well if Rogers hadn't dragged me to the cave up the mountain."

"Be thankful he saved your life."

"I would rather have died fighting the Dragon's forces with my friends. At least I would have died with my dignity."

Tusin sits on a rock and leans against his walking stick. "There is great dignity in caring for those who have lost their lives. Their graves cry out for justice."

"There will be no justice," Starbuck says, eyes flashing and tears forming. "How can there be when there is no army? We have no hope."

"Didn't you say the Wormling told your father he would sing a song of victory when the Dragon is overthrown?"

"He did."

"And does the Wormling lie?"

"He lies dead inside the White Mountain."

"Then perhaps we should retrieve his body and bury it here."

"You know the mountain is probably guarded," Starbuck says, looking at the sky. "And it's only a matter of time before the forces of the Dragon return to kill us."

"How can you be sure?" Tusin says. "How can you know that things spoken by the Wormling will not come true?"

"A wedding? Victory over the Dragon? It's nothing more than a story."

"Didn't he pledge something to you?" Rogers says.

"The Wormling promised my father that he would be by his side when victory came and sing. And here he lies, covered with dirt."

Rogers wanders up the hillside alone and stops at the knoll where Humphrey fell. Humphrey had carried him and Starbuck as he galloped from the Dragon's forces. When the horse fell, Rogers had grabbed Starbuck and scrambled into a cave just as a fiery blast consumed their friends and Humphrey.

The screeching and the burning and the crying of the attack flood over him, and though Rogers puts his hands over his ears, he cannot drown out the sounds, though it has been many days.

Using a crude shovel of wood and stone, Rogers digs a hole beside the horse, and the tears come. Like Starbuck, he had been so filled with hope when he heard stories of the Wormling, and then when he had met him that hope inside rose up like a lion. But now . . .

He digs into the rocky soil until his hands blister and the shovel falls apart. He continues digging until his fingers bleed, crying and clawing and talking to Humphrey and his other friends. He misses the Scribe's voice—crackly and old but full of wisdom. He misses the anger of Connor, who had first yelled the warning of the attack and tried to get his wife, Dreyanna, to safety.

Most of all, Rogers misses Watcher. She was so kind. How anything could harm her, he didn't know. She was the most pure, loving, and sensitive creature he had ever met, yet she was also a fierce warrior. He blinks his tears away, but he cannot blink away the last vision he had of her. She had turned to fight, a mere speck against the enemies arrayed against them. With her ears straight and her back arched, she grabbed a spear from one of Connor's men and aimed it at the heart of a beast flying toward them.

The blast of fire had thrown her onto her back on a rock. Rogers wanted to run to her, but he was galloping away on Humphrey's back. The horse had hesitated when Watcher fell, as if he too had sensed the loss. She reached out toward them. . . .

These images and more run through Rogers's mind the deeper he digs. Night falls and the moon is bright, illuminating his workplace.

Soon he hears footsteps. A fog rises and shrouds the countryside as a lone figure approaches out of the darkness.

Rogers crawls into the hole he dug for Humphrey, picks up a stone, and waits.

17
The Cloaked Figure

The fog drifted up to eerily shroud the visitor like a phantom. Rogers had heard stories (mostly from Starbuck) of evil beings stalking the places of the dead. With this figure walking down the mountain, the moonlight behind him, a hood over his head, Rogers's mind ran wild. Could this be a friend of the Dragon? Had they watched and waited until all the bodies were buried only to attack the living?

Rogers trembled in the hole and gripped the rock. He wished he had gone back to the fire with Starbuck and Tusin before nightfall. At least there he would die with his friends.

The stranger ambled to the edge of the hole. "Dig this yourself?" His voice was strong and compassionate, as familiar as the scent of a meal cooked by someone who loved you.

"Yes," Rogers said, still trembling. "What do you want?"

The stranger knelt and put his hands on his knees, surveying the foggy, moonlit countryside. "What happened?"

"Are you a stranger?" Rogers said. "Have you not heard what the Dragon's forces did to the warriors of the Wormling?"

"Tell me."

"The Wormling told us to leave the White Mountain and we did, just before the Dragon killed him with a blast of fire. No sooner was the Wormling dead than the Dragon amassed his armies against us—before we even had a chance to arm ourselves. They came with fire and venom, and we had no chance."

The stranger scanned the valley, studying the hundreds upon hundreds of graves that rose up in the moonlight. "Did you bury all these yourself?"

"With a few friends," Rogers said. "This is the last, the one who saved my friend and me. We are lucky to be alive."

The stranger moved toward Humphrey, covered with blankets Rogers had taken from other bodies.

"I had to cover him or he would stink," Rogers said.

The stranger—whether from fatigue or emotion, Rogers could not tell—rested his head against the body of the horse and whispered something that drifted off in the night.

"What are you doing?" Rogers said.

"Come up here."

As soon as Rogers had climbed from the pit, the man rolled the horse into the hole without so much as a finger of help from Rogers.

"How strong are you? He weighs a ton."

"It was his heart that was huge," the man said as if he knew Humphrey, and Rogers thought he saw a tear reflected by the moonlight. "You are not lucky, you know," he said.

"Sir?"

"It was not luck that allowed you to survive. There was a purpose."

"Yes, to bury the dead."

"An honorable chore," the man said, filling in the hole around Humphrey's body with the shovel. "But there is more to accomplish."

When the stranger had finished, he patted the earth covering Humphrey and leaned down as if saying a final word to the horse, his chin and mouth visible to Rogers for the first time. "Your future is a bright one, Rogers. Didn't the Wormling say you would be there when he defeats the Dragon?"

"How do you know that?" Rogers said, recoiling.

"Come," the man said. "Take me to your friends."

18

Heartbreak

Owen's heart broke as he walked past the graves of his friends to the camp. Rogers and the others had drawn simple pictures of the people buried there, as these dear ones could not read or write, so deep was the Dragon's hold on them.

Rogers squinted at him as if trying to figure out who this shrouded figure was and whether he could trust him.

Owen crept toward the fire and put his hand on the lad's shoulder. "Don't wake the others. I can see how tired they are. Get some rest and I'll see you at first light."

Owen passed a great mound of earth

under the picture of a massive, bearded man. "Mordecai," he whispered, "this world was not worthy of you. Rest well, my friend. We will meet again."

As the fog lifted, Owen found the graves of Erol and his wife, Kimshi. The weight of the losses hit him hard, and the words of Nicodemus came back to him: *"You are not alone, young prince. Keep the book close until every word is fulfilled. And remember what I have said. No matter what you find—or what finds you."*

Owen found the place where they had laid Watcher. At the head of her small grave were flowers, wrapped into a crude bouquet. The picture did not do her justice, but it had been drawn with love.

"I'm so sorry I wasn't here for you, Watcher. I wish I had seen this coming."

The memory of her voice came back to him. She had been skittish toward him when he first came to the Lowlands. Though she had waited all her life to see a Wormling, he didn't fit the image she must have had of him. She had died without knowing that he was not just the Wormling but the King's Son.

Watcher had confided in him just before he went to the White Mountain that she had lost her power to sense invisibles. Owen had comforted her by quoting *The Book of the King: When the Son comes, he will make everything new again. The old will pass away, and the original order will be restored.*

He had told her in the end, "When I return, you will see the Son."

Now, by the grave, Owen whispered, "I told you to trust me. That your powers would be restored and you would be forgiven." He lay over the grave. "When the King's prophecy is completed, I will see you again. But I thought you would be here and we'd fight the Dragon together."

Owen was alone. His father had left him. Nicodemus, his confidant and protector, was gone. And his dearest, most faithful friend in the Lowlands lay beneath the ground.

Owen fought to breathe through his sobs.

19
Tusin's Breakfast

Tusin awoke to the smell of fish sizzling on the fire. A man in a hood sat with his back to him and turned a spit.

"Hello, friend," Tusin said, hoping he was right.

"Good morning," the man said in a hushed tone as if not to wake the others. "I hope you're hungry."

"Where did you get the fish?"

"Just over the hill," the stranger said. "And I found the skolers growing near the pine grove."

"Amazing," Tusin said. "I've tried to catch fish in that stream for days. And had I known the skolers were there, we wouldn't have been reduced to the berries and plants. . . ." His voice trailed off, and he moved closer to the stranger. "May I ask why you have come to this place?"

"To help."

"You're a little late," Starbuck said, stretching and rising. He headed to the fire, grabbed a skoler, then dropped it and shook his hand, yelping.

The stranger quickly poured water over the burn.

Starbuck muttered something and walked toward the stream.

"He hasn't been the same since his parents were killed. None of us have been the same." Tusin sighed. "Wave after wave of the Dragon's flyers came at us. Those who survived had to face the vaxors. . . ." He closed his eyes, trying to blot the images from his mind. "Some survivors were taken away. I heard one vaxor talk about rebuilding the coliseum.

"Most difficult is that I thought we would be protected. I believed the Wor—" Tusin caught himself before giving away his true allegiance. "I thought someone would come to lead us. But as you can see . . ." He waved across the landscape of graves.

The stranger spoke. "I understand your grief, but you are followers of the true King; are you not?"

Tusin leaned forward, trying to see the man's face. "How

do I know you have not been sent by the Dragon? How do we know you're not here to wipe us from the earth now that we've buried the last of our friends?"

Rogers awoke and stretched. "This is a good man. He helped bury Humphrey."

Batwing alighted on a log not far from the stranger. "What kind of man comes to us with an offering of food?"

"Are you not hungry?" the stranger said. "Do you want something else?"

"Justice, perhaps," Tusin said.

"We do not mean to be ungrateful," Batwing said.

"I understand," the stranger said. "And where is Rotag?"

Tusin looked at him in stunned silence. *How does he know about Rotag?* "There is not enough water here."

"Eat," the stranger said. "We can talk later."

When he handed over the food, Tusin grabbed the man's arm. "Who *are* you?"

With that, the stranger pulled his sword from his scabbard, and Tusin dropped to the ground, quivering. Batwing hovered out of reach. But when the man pulled back his hood and they saw the sad but smiling Wormling, they whooped and shouted and patted him on the back.

"You must tell us everything!" Tusin said. "Where did you go?"

"How did you escape the fire of the Dragon?" Batwing said.

"Where have you been so long?" Rogers said.

"With the help of my friend Mucker, I was able to elude the Dragon at the White Mountain. He thought he had killed me. When I reached the Highlands, I learned of an attack there—"

"The fourth portal," Tusin said, wide-eyed, ahead of the story. "You've breached the fourth portal, haven't you?"

"I've done more than that, my friend," the Wormling said. "I've made a discovery that could change everything."

Batwing said, "What sort of discovery?"

"I could tell you, but I don't want to endanger you. Suffice it to say that the true King is still in control. You must believe this and everything you have heard from *The Book of the King*."

"Read us more," Rogers said.

"Yes!" Batwing said.

"More promises from the book?" Starbuck said, having returned from the river. He stared at the Wormling with fierce eyes. "You told my father he would sing at the defeat of the Dragon. You promised this."

"That is my plan still," the Wormling said.

"How?" Starbuck said. "The voices of my parents cry out from their graves, but no one hears."

"I'm sorry you had to go through this, but I have good news." The Wormling rose to touch his shoulder.

Starbuck stepped back. "Good news in a graveyard?"

"The best news can come from here, for this is not all there is. I once thought that where I lived was all that existed, that only the things I could see and feel were real and the rest was just an illusion. But now I know there is more than we can see and that even those who die can live again through the power of the King."

"How can this be?" Starbuck said. "Can your sword bring a person back from the dead?"

The Wormling placed his hand on the boy's shoulder, and this time Starbuck did not pull away.

"It will take more than a sword, but I have good news. Every word of the King's book will come to pass. Every promise will be kept. And when you are reunited with your family, the joy will be deeper than you've ever known."

"And there will be a wedding," Starbuck said.

The Wormling smiled. "One to end all weddings. And no matter what happens between now and then, you must trust the King. Will you?"

Wings flapped and they all looked up to see Machree, the bird that Watcher and the Wormling had nursed back to health, fly away into the distance.

"I had no idea he survived," Tusin said. "How long could he have been there?"

The Wormling doused the fire with water and soil. "We must leave now. Follow me."

20

The Dragon's
Secret

When telling a story, it is impossible to describe everything or
you would have a book (or in our case, a series) that would never end. Telling a story is like painting a small section of a big canvas and showing what is going on in that tiny part of the bigger world.

However, some parts of our canvas need to be illumined, and many of those portions are quite dark and foreboding, for they tell the depths of deceit to which a heart will plunge. A spotlight on the armies of the Dragon, spread throughout the Lowlands, would show how brutal and uncaring they are. Flying creatures who destroy homes and kill people. Vaxors who overturn furniture, chase families into corners, and plunder valuables. Survivors herded to encampments where they are treated more like livestock than the precious creations they truly are.

Evil does not treat the precious with respect and dignity—rather, it seeks revenge on the creator by mistreating his creation.

On our canvas we could go anywhere—to the Highlands where enemy forces are amassing in attack formation, to the hole in the earth where Mr. Page (the King of the world) has gone, or to where Clara and Connie have retreated—specially prepared by the King himself for just such an attack.

But we must take you to a far, unseen corner of our canvas. Here the Dragon has built a shrine to himself and what he believes will be his eventual reign over the entire created order. It has been heretofore unseen because he has allowed no one into this difficult-to-reach, dank, dreary, Dragon dwelling. Of his council, only RHM knows of its existence, and not even he knows its purpose. Other than him and the Dragon's servants here, only one other living being is aware of this place (we are not counting the captives held here, of course), and we shall meet this being shortly.

The Dragon has slipped away even from those he has

charged with watching his every move, and he now flies high above the Lowlands, grinning and rehearsing what life will be like now that his plans have worked perfectly and his worries are over. All that he has hoped has come to pass, except displaying the Sword of the Wormling on his wall.

There remains but one event that will seal the fate of the enemy of the Dragon, and that is the presentation of the body of the enemy's offspring in the coliseum. Better still would be to feature the enemy's living Son so the Dragon could humiliate and abuse and mistreat this last remnant of the opposition.

This was not all that caused the Dragon's heart to soar as he flew through the murky clouds, scaly wings propelling him toward his secret hideaway. When he had secured the book the vile creature had carried, the Dragon had read how to achieve immortality by using the very words of the enemy. That gave him particular pleasure, because while it was one thing to grind an enemy into the ground like a bug, it was quite another to use the enemy's own weapon against him, whether sword, spear, or words.

The sun faded behind the Dragon, and the red moon rose before him. He had seen a bloody moon only once before— on the night the enemy's Son had been taken from the Lowlands to the Highlands. This had to be a sign that the time of his own ascension had come. Even the moon was worshipping him as the king over all.

The desolate landscape below reminded the Dragon that this area was populated with horrid creatures that lived in freedom but ultimately depended on him for everything. He would herd them all into one place and use them for his amusement.

When the outline of the palace came into view, he blew a blast of fire into the air to announce his approach. From the topmost window came an answering blast, and the Dragon roared.

21

Drucilla

Drucilla groomed herself (if you could call it that) in the dirty glass, batted her eyes, and awaited her beloved. She called the Dragon that because she knew it was what he wanted to hear, but it was not what she felt. With his annihilation of her family long ago, she was thankful she had been allowed to live. At first she had despaired, wondering if life was even worth living, but now she had a reason, and it had nothing to do with her relationship with the Dragon.

He flew onto a parapet and blasted his fire again, as if trying to impress her. She bowed, as any good dragon wife would do, and he entered the upper room.

"My lady," he breathed in a low, gravelly voice, "how lovely you look tonight."

"Thank you," she said. "Are you hungry?"

"Do you still have a supply of villagers in the lower dungeon?" he said.

"A few. But most of them spoiled. A pity. They would have made a good snack."

The Dragon waved. "No matter. When I look at your beauty, it makes my hunger subside."

Truly, we have seen many sickening things in our travels through the kingdom, but perhaps this is the most stomach-turning. The evil beast who has committed violent act after violent act tenderly took the wing of Drucilla and pressed his face to hers, cheek to cheek, in a display of affection. It is good you cannot see this, and we will refrain from describing it further or you might have difficulty ever eating again.

The Dragon pulled back and gazed into Drucilla's eyes. "What news have we of the treasures?"

◆◆◆

Drucilla took the Dragon via the long hallway to the other end of the palace and a door guarded by a long-fanged creature with ripples of muscles and claws that snapped open as soon as something moved in the hallway. It let out a low growl and then roared, the hair on its back standing up.

The Dragon growled as well, startled by the ferocity of the beast.

Drucilla calmed the guard with a soothing tone. "It's all right. We need to look inside a moment."

Inside, three fireplaces were tended by a small, female creature. Stacks of firewood were positioned near the fireplaces, and in the middle of the room sat a wooden trough filled with hay and straw. Atop the straw lay black and brown oblong orbs that seemed to pulsate with the heat.

The Dragon flapped a wing to lessen the heat. "Do you trust that *thing* to watch them?"

"Her life depends on keeping the temperature even in here," Drucilla said. "As do the lives of her family members in the depths."

The Dragon chuckled.

Drucilla brushed a wing over the egg basket as the firelight danced off the sides of them and made eerie reflections on the ceiling and walls. "When I was a little girl, my mother had me watch the hatchlings and make sure the room stayed warm."

"They all hatched?" the Dragon said, feigning interest despite that it was he who had killed Drucilla's family— cutting them down like weeds.

"Only one made it," Drucilla said.

"Don't be sad, my dear," the Dragon droned. "The next generation will grow up and call you the most wonderful mother of all time, for you have brought life to a dream."

She sighed. "To think of them growing up and assisting their father . . ."

"They will rule with honor and make this world even more of an oasis than I will. And their line will be extended—" His eyes grew wide. "Did you see that? One of them moved."

Drucilla leaned close as a portion of the egg jutted but did not crack. "Amazing, isn't it? Step this way and you can see."

Only when he bent and saw the egg by the light of the fire could he detect something small and angular moving around inside the shell.

"That's a wing, I believe," Drucilla said.

"Yes," the Dragon said, more animated. "Astounding! How much longer?"

"Not long," Drucilla said. "And the closer we get, the more I believe that you will be the greatest leader in history."

"Yes, I will," the Dragon said. "My offspring will carry on my vision. I will teach them, and they will become like me."

22

Machree

As we have said, Machree was nursed back to health by the Wormling and Watcher before her unfortunate demise at the hands of the Dragon's army. Having been hidden by the two while he recuperated, Machree was not discovered by the Dragon's forces. And after hearing the conversation of the Wormling and others on the ground, he took flight and headed for the Castle of the Pines.

Before he entered the environs of the Dragon, however, a smaller, brown-winged bird caught up with him and forced him to land in a tree. It was Batwing.

"You would not have survived

without their help," Batwing said. "Would you betray the true King again?"

Machree cawed. "Why do you follow me?"

"I know what you're going to do. Watcher told me what you asked the Wormling to give to you—now you're going to the Dragon to alert him."

Machree looked away.

"You don't know what you're doing. You don't know how evil the Dragon is. He wants to destroy everything the King has worked so hard to give us."

"The *King?*" Machree snapped. "Watch what you say or the one you say is so evil will hear you."

"I'm begging you," Batwing said. "Long ago I tried to tell Tusin and Rotag we should give you another chance, and you do this? Watcher spoke highly of your courage. I can't believe you would betray her memory."

Machree drew closer. "And how did *you* survive? Where were you when the attack came?"

"I was spying, gaining information about—"

"Aha, so you were with the Dragon himself? How convenient. Perhaps you were the one who gave away the location of the army of the Wormling, such as it was."

"You can't be serious."

"Leave me," Machree said. "Before I alert them about you too."

Batwing, tiny compared to Machree and without much power to do anything but fly and spy, gritted his teeth and struggled through the darkness and a southern wind, finally making it over the tree line and disappearing from Machree's sight.

The great bird settled in the treetop, looked toward the Castle of the Pines, and gave an ominous smile, as if he knew something no one else in the Lowlands knew, save one.

23

Dragon City

Owen and his ragtag band of followers were more rag than tag
after walking day and night through
town after town of empty huts and
deserted streets strewn with toys and
belongings—pointing to the quick
withdrawal of the people. Now they
stealthily approached the fortress
known as Dragon City.

Vaxors guarded the four entrances,
so it was impossible to see exactly what
was going on inside, but by leaving his
companions hidden and climbing a
mountain, Owen was able to observe
the construction of buildings and grad-
ing of roads. Horses and oxen did the
heavy lifting, but many workers were

humans. These were no doubt taken from the villages Owen and his group had been through. Owen's heart broke when he saw children forced to help.

He rejoined the others and said, "Since the Dragon's killed our army, he can do what he wants with the others."

"And then throw them into the coliseum for his amusement," Tusin said. "Most of those people are going to be killed by the Dragon's animals. How different the King is. He gives life, but the Dragon saps it from the people."

Owen pulled out *The Book of the King* and read:

> "Near the end of days, the people will be carried away into darkness and made prisoners by the evil one. His amusement will know no end as he constructs his stronghold. But it will not stand. The King comes to give life and life to its full."

"It's almost as if the Dragon has read this and is trying to fulfill it for himself," Tusin said.

Owen nodded. "He wants to prove the King wrong. But he's playing right into the King's hands."

"How so?" Starbuck said. "Those people are not coming out. And all our friends have been killed."

"Things are not always as they seem," Owen said. "If you were to tell the people where I live that the evil of the Dragon exists, they would think you were crazy."

"But *we* know he's real," Starbuck said. "We see the effects every day."

Batwing fluttered and sighed, clearly exhausted from his flight to speak with Machree. Owen had spoken with Batwing briefly about his findings but asked him not to tell the others what he had learned.

"What does that mean for us?" Batwing said. "What do we do now?"

"Keep track of the Dragon's progress," Owen said, "and remember everything that happens inside the city—when they change guards, when work crews come out, where prisoners are held. We need all the information you can gather."

Owen felt breath on his shoulder and turned. Rogers had moved behind him and stood looking at the intricate designs of the book. The boy had a special ability to move almost without being noticed.

"I cannot read anyway, sir," he said. "But why are there pages at the back that have no writing on them?"

Owen flipped to the back. "I used to think this was simply where the missing chapter would go, but now I'm not sure."

"Maybe just extra pages," Starbuck said.

"Nothing the King does is wasted," Owen said. "The pages are here for a reason. We just need to discover what it is."

"What will you do now?" Tusin said. "If we stay here, where are you going?"

Owen closed the book. He had not told them what he had discovered from his study of it while breaching the fourth portal. He had read passages he had seen several times before, but it had only become clear to him during his final trip with Mucker what he was looking for and the consequences if he did not succeed.

"I'm taking Rogers with me, and we will be gone awhile," Owen said.

Rogers's face lit up. Starbuck frowned.

"We have an important mission, and then I'll send word to you. Do not lose heart. No matter what happens, no matter what you hear, no matter what you see, you must trust that all is for the eventual good. Do you understand?"

Tusin and Batwing nodded.

Starbuck seemed confused. "Why does Rogers get to go? Why not me? If it's about what happened back at the valley, I can explain!"

"Please," Owen said, "keep your voice down. It's not because of anything you have done or not done. You had no control over what happened in the valley. Rogers is simply better suited for this journey and mission. You are valued no less than before."

Starbuck hung his head.

Owen put a hand on his shoulder. "You have been through much. You have lost much. But no matter what you have lost, it will be returned to you. Filled to overflowing. What was given up for the cause of the King will be paid back again and again."

Starbuck looked at him, mouth agape, as if Owen were speaking gibberish. "How? Can you bring my family and friends back to life?"

Again Owen looked deeply into the boy's eyes. "'The King will one day dry every eye. Death itself will die. You will have no reason to grieve. You will not experience pain and heart-ache. Open your ears to my words. The things which are now will pass away and that which is new will come.'"

Starbuck's eyes darted. "Is that from *The Book of the King*?"

"It is one of my favorite passages. When I came upon the valley where our friends were buried, I had to look at it again for myself. Do not be ashamed of your anguish. I cried as well. But there is good news for all who follow the King. There is great hope for those who put their trust in him."

24

Flight

When it was dark again, Owen took Rogers up the narrow, winding ridge from where he could see the entire city of the Dragon. He shuddered at the encampment, torches illuminating soldiers reveling in making fun of their prisoners, human and animal alike. It was all Owen could do to keep from charging down upon them with his sword.

"Why have we come here?" Rogers whispered.

Owen held a finger to his lips and looked skyward, whispering, "It's almost time."

The trees fluttered as if some unseen storm were descending upon them.

Owen raised his hands to his mouth and made a noise both scary and wonderful. Soon two large winged creatures landed. Rogers seemed scared of them until Owen introduced them as his friends Grandpa and Petunia.

"How did they know we were here?"

"They know me," Owen said. "They are ready to serve us."

Owen nuzzled Petunia and climbed onto Grandpa's back. Rogers clambered onto Petunia.

Owen leaned close to Grandpa and spoke into one of his huge ears, and they were off.

When out of sight of Dragon City, Grandpa changed direction and Petunia followed, flying away from the moon and everything familiar.

25
A Whispered World

Talea, the girl inside the palace assigned to tend the Dragon's offspring, was young with stubby teeth and flaxen hair that had a mind of its own. Every day of her life had been difficult, and this duty proved no different. Tending to Drucilla's every demand for more wood or less wood was driving her crazy. The eggs were never the right temperature; wind made the room drafty, but the windows needed to be open so fresh air could feed the fire . . . and on and on it went.

Talea toiled so hard for her mistress because she believed she was saving her family. She had left her parents and her older brothers in the dungeon to work in the "nursery."

Beyond reuniting with her family, Talea thought there was no hope for her.

No hope, that is, except for the impossible. No hope, unless it came from outside the palace. Talea believed that no one in the entire kingdom even knew about this dreary place. The shores of the black beach stretched for miles, and rocky crags rose around the palace and gave it the appearance of the very end of the earth.

During the heat of the day, Talea stood with the wooden shutters open, staring out at the endless water and the waves lapping the shore, wondering if this would be where she and her family would die. But something would spring up inside—a feeling that she couldn't describe, much like when her mother had snuggled close to her in the night, whispering tales of times when there had been music, hope for a better world, hope for a future not filled with darkness and dragons and pain. Hope was a whispered world too beautiful to describe, too wonderful to speak of—a future with the true King in control, where you were not imprisoned in some old castle, not ordered about by the only remaining female dragon (and reminded of it every day), and not commanded to care for the next generation bent on the slaughter of her people.

Talea could barely imagine true paradise any more than a

person blind from birth can imagine a sunset. The closest she had come to knowing paradise was through the love of her family. There had been some haunting beauty to the life they shared that spoke of something greater, something just out of their grasp, something in the future that promised *more*.

Drucilla broke Talea's train of thought with a shout.

The girl, gathering the chain by her blackened ankle, moved to the door and peeked into the hallway. "Yes, my lady?"

"Salve the eggs and put fresh logs on the fire," Drucilla bellowed. "Then go to sleep."

"Yes, my lady."

Talea did not know where Drucilla came by such a substance, but it was clearly something dragons believed necessary for the proper nurturing of their young. She tried to breathe through her mouth so the smell wouldn't turn her stomach. This salve—"dragon grease," as she called it—was rancid, like something dead or rotting. She applied it to the pulsating eggs, spreading it evenly over the veined shells. Of all the things Drucilla made her do, this was the most disgusting. But Talea was doing this for her family.

Talea looked away from the horrible eggs and spotted something in the shadows. In the corner a figure moved. She stopped and stared, chin quivering.

"Don't be frightened," the figure said.

26

End of the Earth

In the Highlands it is said that someone will go to the ends of the earth
for a cause. This, of course, does not
mean that there is an end to the earth
but that nothing will stop him from
achieving his goal.

However, in the Lowlands, there
truly was an end of the earth, at least
in terms of a place a person would
never want to go.

As Owen had come through the
fourth portal, he had read a passage
near the end of *The Book of the King*.
With renewed interest he pored over
it, committing it to memory.

Call unto those who are poor, those who are outcast, those who cannot see or hear, the ones who need good news but are left in the throes of despair and don't know that help is on the way. The pain of those who have been cast into ravines of grief has reached the King. Behold, the one who will bring healing to the land has come and will rescue even those who feel beyond hope. They will become shining followers of the King and his Son, helping usher in the new wholeness.

This passage had jogged something, but it wasn't until Owen stood over Watcher's grave that the thread running through his mind connected with words of the past. A conversation with her when they were escaping Connor's wrath came floating back. He had looked into the distance from the Valley of Shoam and asked what lay in the other direction.

Watcher had shuddered and said, "Wilderness as far as you can imagine. And a place known as Perolys Gulch."

"Who lives there?"

"A race of cursed people. Outcasts. Diseased. If ever you even dream of going there, you will go alone."

Owen had been surprised at Watcher's fear. She was usually eager to venture into any setting, no matter the danger, but just the mention of Perolys Gulch had made her voice tremble.

Owen felt pain in his stomach even now at the memory. She had not known she was predicting something that would come true. *"If ever you even dream of going there, you will go alone,"* she had said, and now, on the back of Grandpa, that was exactly what Owen was doing. He grieved Watcher anew, holding on to the hope that he would one day see her again— or that something of her would survive.

He had left Rogers at the Dragon's secret hideout and had given him an assignment, assuring him he could accomplish it and reminding him how important his success was. Owen knew Rogers could slip into any situation undetected, for this was his gift.

The mists rose in the foreboding darkness, and Owen huddled close to Grandpa's back to keep the cold wind from his face. The sun had receded over the horizon behind them where he had first entered the Lowlands, now washed out by the breaching of the Mountain Lake. Trees lay like toothpicks at the bottom of the valley, and he strained to see the home where Bardig and his wife had lived.

As they flew the scenery changed. Owen had ventured through the desert near Erol's home and crossed the Valley of Zior, but he was not prepared for what he saw now. The ground rose and fell in a jagged pattern, and the landscape was filled with rocky crags. He had never seen trees like this—bare bark and no leaves or needles. They looked like twisted sticks, their branches reaching toward the sky like worshippers raising their hands to God for help.

It was so barren—even more so than the desert—that it pained Owen to look at it. He was sure the land had once supported plant life, but now the area looked like something only a Dragon would love.

They flew toward a precipice that overlooked a cavernous valley, and Grandpa pulled his wings up and headed in the opposite direction. Owen guided him back, but once again the transport flyer balked at venturing into the chasm. Speaking gently, Owen coaxed him near a rocky ledge, but though he had developed a great power to influence animals—even the most evil of beasts—he could not get the flyer into the valley.

"All right," Owen said. "I can see you are frightened. Wait for me here."

Grandpa looked back at Owen, and his eyes said, "You will never return."

Owen stroked the beast's flank. "I promise I'll be back."

Talea grabbed a stick from the woodpile. The stranger stayed in the darkness, but she could tell he was shaking. At first she thought he was crying, shrinking in fear, but then she looked closer.

"Why do you laugh?" she said.

When he moved into the light, she stepped back and raised the stick. "Don't come any closer."

"I come with an important message," he said with a deep voice and a wonderful smile.

"I'll scream for Drucilla!"

He held up a hand. She could tell

he was young, and his eyes looked kind and not at all evil like
Drucilla's or the guards'.

"I mean you no harm, princess."

Talea cocked her head. "Princess? Have you come to mock
me? How did you get in here?"

"'Nothing that lasts is ever quickly attained,'" the stranger
said.

She squinted. "What?"

"I did not even know you would be here. But I can tell by
watching that you are decent and trustworthy." His gaze fell
on the chain manacled to her leg. "I was sent to find the eggs
of the Dragon. As for how I got in here, I can only say that
stealth is my gift."

She held up the stick again. "I cannot allow you to get near
those eggs."

He bowed and stepped back. "I have no quarrel with you.
You are an innocent bystander."

"If anything happens to *any* of them, I will die as well as
my mother, father, and brothers."

The stranger bit his lip and looked at the fire. Compassion
showed on his face, though Talea still feared he might lunge
at the eggs.

"Where is your family?" he said.

"In the dungeon. But if I tend these eggs and keep them

safe until they become hatchlings, Drucilla will release my family back to our farm. We can live again in peace."

The stranger clasped his hands as if begging. "I must gain your trust, but I can't do that here. It's crucial that I get you away from this place and that the Dragoness not know of my presence."

"Leave," Talea said. "I won't tell her."

He shook his head. "You don't understand. You are in grave danger. She will never let you live in peace; she will tear you to pieces. You would not understand this danger unless you had heard what the book said. The Wormling told me—"

"Wormling? And what book? Books have been banned here from before I was born."

"I know. Please, now allow me to tell you of—"

The stranger stopped as a *thump, thump, thump* came from the hallway.

"Drucilla," Talea whispered. She dropped her stick and sat quickly on the stool, spreading the foul grease on the eggs. The door swung open, and Talea looked up at Drucilla as if nothing were wrong, but her heart beat furiously, and she wondered if the Dragoness could smell her fear.

"I heard voices," Drucilla said.

Talea stared at the eggs, then back at her mistress. "Voices, Your Majesty?"

The Dragoness's eyes swept the room. No one was there. Talea wondered if the stranger had gone out the window or scurried behind the far fireplace.

Drucilla summoned a guard and asked if he had heard anything.

"The girl talks to herself, perhaps to the eggs," he said.

Drucilla turned back to Talea. "My babies need their rest if they are to grow into strong young dragons. Do not speak to them or do anything to disturb them. It won't be long until they see their father."

"Yes, Your Highness."

When Drucilla marched away and the door closed, Talea whispered, "Are you still here?"

The stranger moved, and she was amazed at how he had blended in with the stone walls. "Yes. Thank you for not alerting her."

Talea wiped her hands and leaned toward him, speaking just loud enough to be heard. "Who is this Wormling, and what does he have to do with me?"

"Oh, he is wonderful! You would love him. He has come here from a place where books are read at will and stories pass from parent to child. Songs too."

"It *does* sound wonderful. But why would a person who lives there come here?"

The stranger crept closer. "That's the best part. He

The Stranger

was given *The Book of the King* and has read beautiful passages to me. He was sent to help us and the people of his world."

Talea's eyes brightened. "The writing of the true King is in the book?"

"Yes."

Finally they introduced each other and shook hands, Rogers telling her, "My parents were killed by the Dragon. I have sworn allegiance to the King, his Wormling, and his Son, who is soon to return."

"My father has talked about that," she said. "Please, you must get this Wormling to save my family."

"That is not my role here. The Wormling gave me a specific charge to locate the eggs of the Dragon and then wait for him."

Talea cocked her head. "How could the Wormling know the Dragon had a mate and eggs? That seems impossible."

"He told me he found clues in the book. Words he did not understand—could not understand until now."

"And where is he?"

Rogers looked away. "He wouldn't say, but he was quite solemn when he left."

Talea grabbed Rogers's sleeve. "I cannot wait for him. You must help me. You must rescue us. Surely this Wormling is kindhearted and would want you to."

"I'm sure he would," Rogers said. "But if I act too soon, I could frustrate his plans. I must wait for him."

Talea's mind raced. "Then do this. Go to the dungeon and locate my family. Get word to them that help is on the way."

Rogers stared into her eyes. "That I can do, princess."

If you have ever climbed a mountain without a rope to make sure
you do not splatter if you fall, you will
understand how Owen felt descending a treacherous crevasse. With each
step and slippery handhold, he moved
closer to a fog-shrouded area he could
not see through.

Owen's foot slipped, sending rocks
cascading down the side. He hung
there, listening for the strike of the
rocks against the floor of the canyon,
but it was either a bottomless pit or so
deep he couldn't hear the impact. He
pulled himself up to a ledge, catching
his breath, stilling his heart, choking
back the panic.

What would happen to the Lowlands if I never came out of this abyss? Is there some backup plan by the King? Am I still protected by some other being—a stand-in for Nicodemus—or am I totally on my own?

To keep fear at bay, Owen immediately brought to mind several passages from *The Book of the King. Strength is chosen* caused his heart to soar. *To act in fear is to admit you do not know the truth,* another passage said. *A true follower of the King will respect him and fear no other.*

As a trickle leads to a creek, a creek to a stream, a stream to a river, and a river to the sea, Owen's thoughts turned from fear to his father.

Another memorized passage reminded him of the Queen, his mother—her goodness, her wisdom, and her care. *The love and compassion of the Son's mother reach to the ends of the Lowlands and restores the broken and beaten and bruised. The outcast will receive the comfort of her presence.*

This was why Owen was descending this precipice even now, carefully measuring each step. The book foretold not only good and pleasant and hope-filled things but also those that caused tears and questions and the stomach to clench. Everything in Owen told him his mother had been sentenced to this place of the downtrodden and forgotten. His heart had been set on this rescue ever since his trip from the Highlands. But a passage kept coming back to him, one he had not mem-

orized, so before he reached the fog below, he sat on a shelf
and pulled the book from his pack.

> Do you seek someone wise—an intelligent, learned person? The King has taken the understanding of the most respected and has shown it to be silly. Even the silliness of the King is wiser than anyone who thinks himself smart. The King's weakness will overcome the enemy's strength, for he chooses to use the weak, the weary, the lowly, and the despised so no one may be prideful. Indeed, the enemy will fall by the hand of the King, who works through those with no voice, those with no standing, and those in exile.

Owen closed the book and continued, entering the white
mists as he mulled over the passage. Soon his footsteps
echoed, so he called out and his voice returned too. He
stopped, thinking he might be next to a parallel canyon wall.
He squinted but could make out nothing through the thick,
white soup.

Owen's first impulse was to continue, however (and this has
been such an important word throughout the short life of the
Wormling), for some reason unknown to him, he hung there
and waited. When the fog showed no signs of dissipating, he
shouted to Grandpa, pleading with him to enter the chasm.

His voice echoed so loudly that Owen wanted to clamp his
hands over his ears, but that is unwise when clinging to the

JERRY B. JENKINS † CHRIS FABRY

side of a mountain. He yelled again, this time commanding the flyer to descend, but again there was no response.

Finally, holding on with both hands, he used his right foot to test the next level and found there was none. Suddenly, his left foot slipped and he dangled perilously.

"Grandpa!" Owen shouted. "I need you now!"

His arm strength ebbing and unable to find purchase with either foot, Owen was quickly running out of options. He could let go and hope the drop was short. Or he could swing himself to the other side and try to grab the wall that must be there. Something, after all, was making his voice echo. Either option required a great leap of faith, but the latter seemed better than dropping until plopping.

He was about to leap to the other side when he heard a *whoosh* and then a *kerflaaaap* and then another *whoosh*. Grandpa's spindly legs appeared overhead, and his out-stretched wings sent the fog billowing just enough to reveal that the wall that would have been Owen's destination was but a thin veneer of rock that surely would have broken off with his weight. And below? A cavern so deep that Owen's mouth dropped at the sight of it.

However (again this great word), directly below him lay about two feet of open space before a short ledge that led to a pathway. All Owen had to do was drop onto this ledge without falling over the side.

Do not doubt in the dark what you know is true in the light sprang to Owen's mind from the book. The light was soon gone, because as quickly as he had arrived, Grandpa screeched and lifted away, leaving the fog to settle around Owen again. He let go, reached the sand on the pathway, and landed on his seat, thankful he hadn't swung out into the abyss.

"Who goes there?" a gruff voice said. "Answer or you're dead."

Rogers had assumed that some
weird *being* would be watching
the Dragon's eggs, if not the Dragoness
herself, certainly not some pretty, doe-
eyed girl he would feel sorry for the
moment he saw her.

"Locate the eggs or hatchlings," the
Wormling had said. "Find out who is
watching them and wait for my return."

Rogers suspected the girl was a
decoy—that she might have even been
a Changeling there to attack anyone
attempting to harm the eggs. It didn't
appear so, but how could he know?

Rogers had accomplished quite a

feat just getting to the secret chamber where the eggs were kept. Now he crept onto the balcony of the palace, right outside the window, and worked his way down by stepping in the cracks of the stones. The cracks had grown fewer and farther between, and he felt vulnerable on the wall with invisibles and scythe flyers darting about.

Finally he found a channel into the balcony below, then slipped inside and down the stairs where there were fewer guards. You may wonder how Rogers could do such a thing, but, as we have said, everyone has a gift and Rogers's was stealth. He was surreptitious and able to elude detection. Plus, none of the guards stationed here by the Dragon believed anyone would find the place or risk entering such a well-kept fortress if they did.

Rogers sneaked past sleeping guards and those more interested in their food until he came to a thick, locked door. A rank odor, pungent with mildew and something rotten, made him wonder if the cooks had left their potatoes inside this room too long.

Rogers peeked through the keyhole, but the other side was dark. He put his mouth over the opening and whispered, "Anyone in there? Can anyone hear me?"

He heard only the distant roar of water hitting the shore outside and the *drip, drip, drip* of the damp halls.

"Hello?" he called a little louder, his voice echoing. He

held his breath, expecting suspicious footsteps, but none came.

Then through the murky darkness came a grunt and a stirring of water.

Rogers strained to see through the keyhole. "Can you hear me?" he tried a little louder.

Rogers ripped a piece of cloth from his shirt and held it to a torch on the wall. The cloth lit, and he dangled it in front of the keyhole. All that served, of course, was to illumine his face for whoever was on the other side. He jumped high enough to toss the burning cloth through the opening above the door, then peered through the keyhole again.

Through the faint flickering, Rogers saw long, gray hair and an eyeball. "Get us out of here," a man said in a raspy voice.

"Are you Talea's father?" Rogers said.

"Talea?" the man said. "I don't know any Talea." A pause. "Oh, Talea. Yes, she's my daughter."

Rogers frowned. "Don't lie to me. I will help you, but I must find Talea's family."

Another voice, feminine and older, said, "I know her family. Their cell is below us, through the passage."

"Then there is hope," Rogers whispered.

Something moved behind him. A guard sent his hot, smelly breath onto the back of Rogers's neck. "So, you got out of there, did you?" the beast growled. "Well, back in with you."

I come in peace," Owen said quickly.
"I've come to help."

"We have everything we need."

"Except your freedom," Owen
said. "Let me talk to your leader. Your
council or magistrate. Whoever is in
charge. Perhaps your queen."

Owen heard a wheeze, then a long
pause. Through the fog, a withered,
skeletal hand pocked with white and
dark splotches reached for him.

Owen stepped back to the edge of
the precipice. The hand retreated into
the fog.

"I'll come with you," Owen said.

"What weapon do you have?" the
being said.

"A sword. But it is sheathed. I mean you no harm."

"If you mean us no harm, give it to me."

Owen had sworn he would never give up his sword again, but he wanted to show these people he was a friend.

Suddenly a man's face shot out, inches from Owen's, with long, stringy, dirt-filled hair that hung past his chin. The whites of his eyes were so large and the pupils so small that they looked like black olives in the middle of gigantic snowballs. The skin was sallow and stretched to the breaking point, and the lips had pulled back to reveal teeth like icicles with large gaps. The chin jutted out like a pier on the ocean. The man's nose had worn away, leaving just stubbles of cartilage. A black hat lay low on his forehead, and his shirt and pants bore massive holes. Owen glanced at the man's bare feet, little more than flesh drawn tight over bones.

Owen unsheathed his sword with a zing, and the man's mouth dropped open, exposing a shriveled tongue.

"Is it magic?" the man said.

"Take it," Owen said.

Skeleton Man held Owen's sword
as high as he could with his skinny
arms, sending the fog away to reveal
a world of caverns cut into rock walls.
It reminded Owen of Erol's home,
but this was much more barren, and
instead of the caves forming above, they
descended into a rock-strewn walkway.

"Why have you come here?" the man
said, nudging Owen into the compound.

"To help," Owen said. "And to ask
for help."

The man laughed as if he had gargled
razor blades. "*Our* help? We have nothing but disease to offer, and neither will
you if you are exposed to us too long."

"We'll see about that."

As they moved along, people emerged and lined the pathway. They wore large hats or hoods and scarves around their faces. Any patches of exposed skin were either totally white or as dark as tar. The people waved crooked sticks as Owen passed, shouting from spent lungs.

"A pure one is here!"

"He won't be pure for long!"

"Rather cute! Come here, prince!"

Owen kept a careful eye on Skeleton Man, who could not hold the Sword of the Wormling aloft for more than seconds at a time. Finally he just let it drag.

"How did you get here, pure one?" he said. "Sentenced by the Dragon?"

"I came of my own free will," Owen said.

"Don't lie to me!" the man shouted.

Owen heard a zing and ducked just in time to avoid his own sword. It clanged on a large rock and landed in a thicket of gnarly twigs.

"How dare you mock us like that?"

"I'm telling the truth," Owen said, retrieving the sword. He scratched himself on a thorn, and blood pooled on his skin. He handed the weapon back to the man, smiling. "Now be careful with that."

Skeleton Man just stared at Owen's scratch. "We no longer bleed. We no longer have feeling at all."

156

"And this happened after you came here?" Owen said.

He shook his head. "Long ago the Dragon gave us this curse when we lived in the Amoyn Valley and the Valley of Shoam and a hundred other hamlets. Anyone with the disease was forced to flee here or the rest of the people would catch it as well. The Dragon sent a special battalion of flyers to carry us. Then he destroyed those flyers so we had no hope of escape."

No wonder Grandpa wouldn't come. He must have known.

"As for food, what little we get is dropped from the sky— meat unfit for vultures. Only the insane would come here of their own free will. Or someone ignorant."

"Well, I assure you I am neither insane nor ignorant. What is your name, friend?"

"Thaddeus, and I'm not your fr—"

"Take me to the Queen."

"How do you know the Queen is here?" Thaddeus said, slowly raising the sword again, arms quivering. "You must be an agent of the Dragon. He is the one who sent her to us."

"I'm the enemy of the Dragon, and I've met the Queen before. Trust me. She'll want to see me."

Thaddeus limped along, dragging the sword until Owen offered to carry it. So winded that he was gasping, he easily gave it over. "She is the first among us without the disease, so we lodge her as far from us as possible. We have this wild

notion, you see, that there might be hope for her rescue
one day."

Owen stopped. "That's why I am here but not just for her.
You will provide aid, and the King will give you strength to
accomplish great things."

"Like standing for more than a few minutes? being able to
lift a stone?"

"Don't mock the King's power, Thaddeus. *The Book of the
King* says, 'You have not seen nor heard, nor has an inkling of
what is to come entered your heart. But the King is preparing
something marvelous for you.'"

"*The Book of the King?* What has that to do with us
outcasts?"

"It applies to everyone who embraces it," Owen said. "You
do not have to live like this or stay here. The King loves outcasts. He will lift you from this place."

"You speak fairy tales."

"He sent the Queen to you, didn't he?"

"She did not come of her own accord. She was sentenced
here."

Owen faced Thaddeus, eyes flashing. "You wouldn't even
believe if the Son of the King himself were to visit you."

"Not true!" Thaddeus yelled. "That would be different. But
the Dragon would never let him live."

Owen stared at Thaddeus until the man looked away.

32
Survivors

Rogers fell into a smelly pit of water up to his neck, finding himself in a hallway leading to the now submerged cells. He coughed and sputtered and shook himself as he trudged up a ledge.

Hearing whispers in the darkness, he said, "I'm looking for Talea's family. I need information. Who knows them?"

More whispers.

". . . from the Dragon . . ."

". . . don't think we can trust him . . ."

". . . kill him . . ."

"Think again," Rogers said. "The Wormling sent me."

"Wormling?"

"He's come?"

Rogers didn't want to say that the Wormling had come, been presumed dead, and returned again. That he had come once was hard enough to believe. "The Wormling told me himself that the Son is coming. And when the Son returns, his light will spread throughout the land. No place will be left untouched."

"The Dragon has touched every part of the land," a man said, his voice raspy. "How will the Son defeat him?"

"With the words of the King. Not one prophecy will be left unfulfilled. Everything in *The Book of the King* will come true."

"We can't even read!" a woman said.

"The Wormling has never done a thing for us."

"Why would the Wormling allow you to get locked up here if he's so powerful?"

"It wasn't his fault," Rogers said. "I was trying to help a friend find her family and was spotted."

"None of them are alive," a woman said. "Your friend's family did not make it out of the flood. We were the only ones let out of our cells when the water came."

Rogers's heart fell. Talea served the Dragoness for the distinct purpose of saving her family. How would he tell her they were gone? How could he persuade her to continue her work until the Wormling returned?

If the water rose again, Rogers would surely die too. And even if it didn't, how could he wait for the Wormling as he had been instructed? He couldn't even get back to Talea with the awful news.

33
Weak Protection

O wen followed Thaddeus through the ghastly cave village, and more people came out and pushed close to him.

Thaddeus motioned them back. "He is a pure one," he kept saying. "Don't touch him."

The people stared at Owen as if he were an alien. Older ones, barely able to walk, squinted from their resting places. Others gazed passively while munching miserably on what looked like bark.

In the midst of a group of people wrapped in shawls and ragged blankets was a girl not more than ten years old, her head shaved.

Owen fixed his eyes on her and stopped. When he knelt and smiled at her, many fell back. He spoke softly. "Why are you here?"

Her eyes sparkled, but she turned and called for her mother.

The woman gathered her in and glared at Owen. "What do you want with us? We don't need your kind."

"What *kind* is he?" a woman said, her voice floating down the rocks and reaching into Owen's heart.

With a start he shaded his eyes and looked up to a lone dwelling high above the floor of the gulch, where the Queen stood on a ledge.

People seemed to appear from everywhere, whispering, calling to others, pointing.

Thaddeus bowed and took off his hat, exposing his splotchy, grotesque head, but the Queen did not turn away. "Your Highness, I was hunting the east quarter in the fog and heard wings. But instead of meat falling, I found this young man who claims he has met you before."

"What is your name?" the Queen said, her head high.

"Your Highness," Owen said, "I met you at the mine when you were in the separation room. I am the Wormling."

The people gasped and murmured.

The Queen edged forward. "You are either an impostor or your appearance has greatly changed."

Owen pulled out his sword and raised it. "I have been through much since last I saw you, Your Highness. My appearance may have changed, but this should tell you all you need to know. It is the Sword of the Wormling. And in my pack is *The Book of the King.*"

"Stay where you are," the Queen said as Owen moved closer. "You were going to search for my Son. Did you find him?"

Owen stared at his mother, knowing that the mirror of her in the Highlands was Mrs. Rothem. He could see the same kindness in her eyes. "I did find him," he said haltingly. "And I also spoke with your husband. He met me in the Highlands."

She put a hand to her face. "The King is alive?"

"I'm coming up," Owen said.

The Queen shook her head. "Stay where you are. Anything you have to tell me you can say in front of these people."

Owen scanned the growing crowd gazing up at the Queen as if she were some beacon of hope—their only reason to keep going. *Enough for a decent army,* Owen thought. *Wounded warriors but an army nonetheless.*

He broke for the stone stairway, and several men hobbled to block him. Owen skirted them, jumped to the fifth step, and continued.

The people shouted and threw stones, but they were too

weak to even come close. A few men tried to follow, but halfway up they were overcome with fatigue.

"Stay away from me!" the Queen shouted when Owen reached the top.

"Don't worry. I don't have their disease."

Owen wanted to run to her and embrace her and tell her the truth, but she ran into the cave.

When he unsheathed his sword, the crowd yelled for him to stop and hurled threats.

Owen held it high. "This is the Sword of the Wormling given to me by the King of the Lowlands, who is also King of the Highlands and the creator! Do not be afraid! This sword will lead you to victory over the evil one!"

Owen crept into the woman's dwelling to find nothing but a straw mat and a blanket. No table. No chair. No vanity with a mirror. And no food but a half-eaten piece of rancid meat. The Queen kept her back turned to him, and it was all Owen could do not to run to her. She was much thinner than when he had last seen her, and no wonder.

Owen had grown much through his travels and adventures, but the truth was he still longed for her embrace, for the warmth and security that only a mother can give.

"Your Highness," he said, "you need not fear me. I am not diseased. There is something I must tell you. Something you'll want to hear."

"Stay where you are," she said, wringing her hands and pacing.

"The King gave me a message for you," Owen said, his voice cracking.

She turned and glanced at him, then turned back again. "How am I to believe you?"

"I saw him in the Highlands. He has found Gwenolyn."

The Queen reached for the wall to steady herself. "My daughter is alive?"

"And beautiful, like you."

She waved as if the news was too much. Finally, she said, "Swear to me my husband and my daughter are all right."

"Gwenolyn is fine. She's taking Onora to a safe place. Onora was stung by the minions of time."

The Queen faced him. "You're saying the bride still lives too?"

He nodded. "I assume they're still safe, of course. The King took every precaution."

"Always. Except for me."

"Oh, don't say that. He *did* think of you. He told me as much." Owen recounted the King's words. "He said he knew you had been treated badly and that things would get even worse for you. But he also said your life would not be taken."

"It might as well have been," she said.

"Not true. A flyer who can take us out of here awaits above."

The Queen turned away again, and her shoulders shook.

"I don't blame you for losing hope," Owen said softly. "And neither did the King. He said you would despair and that the Dragon would test you in every way, but you're a woman of uncommon courage and strength."

"The King thinks more highly of me than he ought. I have betrayed him in a thousand ways, believing he abandoned me."

Owen moved closer and reached to touch her but held back. Like a mighty river pushing at swollen banks, his emotions fought to overwhelm him. Through tear-filled eyes he saw her glance at him.

"I know who you are," she whispered. "I knew as soon as you left the mountain that day. Your face, the resemblance to your father, the way you spoke—everything confirmed what I knew in my heart."

Owen staggered to embrace her, but the Queen blocked him.

"Mother, I told you—I don't have the disease. You don't have to worry."

She shrank back, finally uncovering her face to reveal a white spot on her cheek. "I'm not worried about me. I'm worried about you."

35

The Stain

"Since I arrived, I've wanted to help these people," the Queen sobbed. "I gave them hope that someone could live in their midst and not be tainted by the disease, but now I have become one of them."

Owen could stand it no longer and embraced his mother. She pleaded with him to let her go, but Owen hugged her all the more and cried with her.

"I have dreamed of this day," she managed, looking Owen full in the face.

"I have as well," he said, wiping his tears. "And seeing you like this makes me wonder what I could have done to keep you from this."

The Queen cupped his face. "Surely you have read what your father wrote. 'Pain is part of the recipe of life.' I was chosen for this and will accept it."

"But if only I had—"

She shushed him. "Our lives are not about getting everything right. We stumble and fall. Difficult paths lead to what is good. Your father asks you to choose what is good and true. And when you do that, you can't help but change the lives of those around you and fulfill his purpose for you."

Owen sat, elbows on his knees, smiling sadly. "When I was younger, I would come across a passage in a book about a mother and her child, and I would dream about what my own mother would say to me."

Owen told her all about the bookstore, Mr. Reeder, books that thrilled him, his school, his few friends—in short, everything he could remember about the Highlands. Then he quoted passages from *The Book of the King*.

The Queen's eyes filled. "It's like listening to *him*. His words bring fire to my heart."

"It will bring more than that," Owen said.

A noise outside interrupted him, and his mother quickly covered herself and led him to the entrance.

Thaddeus, hat in hand, called up to them in his hoarse voice. "Your Highness, we thought we heard crying and wanted to make sure you were all right. Has he hurt you?"

Owen whispered in his mother's ear, and she nodded. She lifted both hands. "My friends, I have news for all afflicted with the disease that has brought you here. The Wormling has come!"

Faint cheers and applause came from people too weak to make much noise. Word had spread, for the amphitheater was packed and more people streamed through the pathways.

"He has met with the true King," the Queen continued. "He is a young man of the book—*The Book of the King*. His message is one of life and hope for the future."

"What future?" Thaddeus said. "I mean you no disrespect, Highness, but we have no future. We will die here."

"I implore you," the Queen said, "to listen to him." She rolled up her sleeves to expose her whitened skin. "Listen to what he has to say to *us*."

The crowd wailed, "It's our fault! You're sick because of us!"

"Please," she said, "this is the not the end." But the people's laments drowned her out. She held up her hands and waited. Finally, when they had quieted, she said, "Thaddeus, what do you desire more than anything?"

Owen could hardly contain himself as the man struggled to find the words. It was as if he hadn't even dared desire anything for so long that he hardly knew where to begin. Finally, lips quivering, he said, "To be clean!"

"Yes!" someone shouted.

"To be spotless!"

"To be pure!"

Thaddeus seemed to feed off the crowd, standing taller now. "And I long to return to my home and the land where we grew crops and fed our children. Yes! To live without fear!"

"To have our lives back!"

"To see my family again and to embrace them!"

"To take off my hood!"

"To not be ashamed!"

A flood of voices filled the amphitheater, the people so busy shouting they didn't notice Owen walking down the steps and joining them. When the thunder of noise subsided, the people swarmed him. He took out his sword and drew a large circle in the sand.

"What are you doing?" the little bald girl said.

Owen put a hand on her head and leaned close. She wrapped her arms around his neck, and the people looked terrified.

"Do you want to be healthy again?" Owen said.

"I can't remember what it feels like," the girl said.

"Look at me," Owen said, showing his arms to the crowd. "The King offers freedom from your condition if you will only receive it."

A woman scowled. "How can you offer the impossible?"

"Only the King has the power to cleanse you," Owen said.

"The truth is, even those who appear healthy have stains within."

"What do you mean?" Thaddeus said.

Owen opened *The Book of the King*. "'Everyone is contaminated by the enemy's stain. On some it is easily seen, but in others the stain is hidden. So then, if all have this stain, how will they be cleansed? How can they be pure again?'"

The people seemed mesmerized.

An echo of a voice came to Owen's mind. *"Your wound is your strength."* He slipped off a shoe and sock.

The people pressed close, clearly amazed at the hue of his skin compared to theirs.

"The enemy comes to kill you from the inside out," Owen said. "He wants to steal the pleasure of living. His desire is to destroy." He raised the sword and looked up at his mother. "But the book says the King has promised life to anyone who wants it. He wants you to live your lives to the full."

Many shook their fists at him, but others looked on earnestly.

Owen asked for a bowl and was handed a stone basin used to catch rainwater. He brushed off his foot and showed the scar from where Mr. Page (also the King) had cut him to remove the locator the Dragon had implanted.

The people fell back when Owen used his sword to slice his foot open, and blood spurted from it into the bowl. He motioned for his mother to come down.

36

Conflict in
the Highlands

Clara closed the door to Connie's room and tiptoed along the dark hallway of their hideout—an aged bed-and-breakfast called the Shadow Inn. The King had rented all the rooms and told her in the letter he had given her that all her meals would be taken care of as well as care for Connie. But the proprietors, an elderly couple, offered burnt toast for breakfast, nothing for lunch, and peanut-butter-and-jelly sandwiches for dinner.

"My friend is sick," Clara had told them the night before, trying in vain to get more food and some aspirin for

Connie. "My father will not like the way you're treating us. He paid you well."

The man shrugged. "Tell your father to come back and complain."

The next night the woman sat back and warmed her hands with a coffee mug as Clara approached the kitchen. The place was worse than drafty, the upstairs rooms so cold you could see your breath. Clara wondered why the couple had not been stung by the minions. There were certainly enough holes in the walls and windows.

"I heard screams outside," Clara said. "What's going on?"

"Nothing new," the woman said. "Lots of people have been stung and—"

"Not that," Clara said, opening a curtain. "It sounds like an attack. Noise from the sky . . ." A light flashed. "Did you see that?"

"It's just a storm," the woman said, cackling. "You kids watch too many horror movies."

Clara noticed a flickering streetlight at the end of an alley and two figures facing each other. One was clearly the proprietor, built squat with fat arms, a protruding belly, and hair that stuck out of the back of his undershirt. The other wore a hooded cloak and stayed in the shadows.

"Get away from that window!" the old woman ordered. "Lightning can knock you across the room." Her tone softened. "I once had an aunt who was at the screen door when lightning struck and . . ."

Clara moved but could still see through the opened curtain. The light went out at the end of the alley. Seconds later lightning flashed, and she caught her breath. The old man was returning, but the hooded figure just stared at the window. At Clara.

With the next flash of lightning, the figure disappeared.

Clara whirled on the woman. "Who was your husband meeting?"

"I don't know what you're—"

"You're working with them, aren't you?"

"*Them?*" The woman stood and pushed back from the table. Something was wrong with her eyes. Was it Clara's imagination or did they look red?

Clara ran and burst through a door underneath the stairs, tripping and landing on plastic, lumpy and squishy. Human eyes stared back at her from inside the plastic.

The real owners!

The woman behind her chuckled. "Those two just didn't work out."

The other impostor, the one who looked like the husband, came through the back door, his hands gnarled into claws.

Clara leaped to her feet and raced upstairs, the two watching her and laughing as if there was nothing she could do.

She flew down the dark hallway to Connie's room, only to find a hulking form standing over her sleeping charge.

"Leave her alone!" Clara yelled. "I'm the one you want."

The being turned, appearing part human with long hair and a pointed nose. She had seen this man outside the restaurant where she worked. He was a street person called Karl. However, Karl had never looked like this. The other part of him was hideous—like some giant insect. Liquid dripped from his mouth, burning a hole in the floor so big she could see to the basement.

"I know who you are," he growled, eyes glowing. "I've been watching you."

His voice crawled up and down her skin like a thousand cockroaches. Everything in Clara wanted to run and not look back. But something came to her, something her father had said: *Do not think that you are lesser than the Son, for you are chosen as well, a daughter of the King. Chosen because your heart is clean and pure. And because you will one day rise above your fear.*

She had been slow to believe she was a princess, but she had never felt at ease with her parents, never felt she really belonged with them or to them.

The King had explained as much as she could handle— what her real mother was like, how much her parents had both missed her and wanted her back. He also assured Clara that there was no fight she could ever enter in which he would not be there to assist her.

"Your brother was born to gain the victory over the evil one," the King had said. "There is no mirror for him. But there is for you. Remember that when you face the coming evil."

She had told him she didn't understand. But she did now.

"This is the chosen one," Karl said. "And I've been sent to bring her back."

"Get away from her," Clara said, grabbing a heavy brass candlestick from the mantel.

"She will awaken in the Dragon's realm," Karl hissed. "As will you, the last trace of the Dragon's enemy."

With all her might, Clara swung the candlestick and plunged it into the mass of cartilage in his head. Tissue gave way like a crab's legs being snapped, and Karl glared at her as he slumped to the floor.

Connie's ancient, wrinkled skin felt cold and clammy, but Clara could see the slow rise and fall of her chest.

"Connie, we need to leave," Clara said. When Connie did not respond, Clara lifted her from the bed and headed downstairs.

37

Preoccupied

The Dragon's aide noticed that
the Dragon had become preoccupied. With what, RHM did not know,
but it was clear something was afoot.
When the Dragon disappeared for yet
another long stretch, RHM assumed
his leader was perhaps raiding towns,
assisting the vaxors in wiping out every
village between Dragon City and the
Amoyn Valley. But lead vaxor Velvel
had recently announced that all the
villages had been dealt with and that
only a few citizens had escaped into
the caves and hillsides.

"Everyone else is either lying in
their own blood or in His Majesty's
prisons," Velvel said. "When the

stragglers have returned, we will make one more sweep and wipe them out."

"Excellent," RHM had said, pondering the flight of the Dragon. Where was he? What secrets did His Majesty keep from RHM? And why? Didn't he trust him? Was he hiding something at this new palace?

When RHM had dared inquire of the Dragon about these clandestine trips, the beast had snarled and muttered something under his sulfurous breath about "insubordinate workers" and that RHM needed to "keep your dirty tentacles to yourself."

RHM had long desired the authority of his leader, to take over and be the most powerful being in the Lowlands. But that would come in good time when the Dragon grew old and feeble and had no one else to whom to pass his mantle.

RHM contemplated sending a spy to shadow the Dragon, but he had no one he could trust. If his scheme was found out, both the spy and RHM would be incinerated. He had already outlived any other aide the Dragon had ever employed.

A sentry reported spotting wings in the distance. RHM climbed to the top of the castle to watch the Dragon's descent. For some reason, this time the Dragon looked glorious, swaying in the air as if actually enjoying his flight.

As he neared the castle, the Dragon belched fire on the flag of the former resident and consumed it. He plopped down on the parapet next to RHM and gave another blast as sentries and workers gathered in the courtyard and cheered. This was hardly their choice, of course, but rather something the Dragon had had RHM command them to do each time he returned.

"Welcome back, sire," RHM said, probing the Dragon's face for any clue to where he might have been. "Did you have a nice trip?"

"Quite. What news do you hear from Dragon City? Is everything ready?"

"The prisons are full, Your Highness. The vaxors plan one final thrust through the land, and the animals you requested for the coliseum have been procured from the farthest reaches of the kingdom."

"The tigren?"

"Yes. Several."

"And the crocs?"

"They were able to capture only one, but it is magnificent, monstrous, with long, sharp teeth."

The Dragon slammed his tail on the edge of the parapet, knocking stones loose and nearly sending RHM to his death. "I told you I wanted many of those slimy beasts for the center pit in the arena! They are to tear my opposition to pieces!"

"We could have gone with several smaller ones," RHM whined, bowing, "but you'll like this beast. Three sentries died just trying to subdue it."

"Well, why didn't you say so?" the Dragon said. "Perhaps one ferocious croc will be better than a whole pool full of them, eh? Give the victims the idea they might have a chance."

"Exactly, sire, and then the teeth clamp down and—"

"Stop! You're making me want to push up the opening ceremonies."

"Well," RHM said with great pomp, "all the creatures have been delivered to the coliseum, and every human not cowering in the rocks somewhere is in the prison."

The Dragon clicked his talons together. "I want to make sure everyone in the arena will be able to see each falling body—a tribute to my power and authority."

"We have taken care of everything, sire. We are ready to begin the ceremony on any day of your choosing."

The Dragon smiled. "One week from today. And I want a trophy to show the audience."

"Trophy, Highness?"

"The chosen damsel from the Highlands," the Dragon purred. "I promised the king and queen of the west that her blood would anoint my throne."

38

Water Everywhere

Deep in the bowels of the palace, Rogers rubbed his swollen feet. Over the past few days he had attempted to lure one of the guards into the cell so he could subdue him and escape, but the closest any came was when they pushed the daily ration of soggy bread through a small hole under the door. Others had beaten him to it the first few times, but Rogers had finally managed to get a few morsels.

The bigger problem, of course, was water. It was everywhere but not fit to drink. He caught a few handfuls from what dripped from the ceiling, but he needed more.

Rogers could tell the others were perturbed with him because he wouldn't tell them any more about the Wormling. He had said too much already, for what if someone told the Dragoness and she told the Dragon?

Rogers had felt he was doing the right thing when he tried to help Talea find her family. But he realized that was not his mission, and now here he sat, having failed the Wormling.

Heavy footsteps descended the stairs.

One of the people sloshed close to the door. "Two guards," he whispered. "It's not feeding time. What could they want?"

"Shh! Listen."

"They're talking among themselves. Something about the Dragoness wanting a snack."

"No!" a girl hissed. "I'm the smallest. They'll pick me."

"No, give them him!" someone said. "The new guy."

Rogers tried to back away, but three people were already on him. "Stop it!" he said. "What are you doing? I'm here to help you!"

As the door opened, they threw Rogers at the feet of the guards.

"We need something smaller," a guard said. "Isn't there a young girl still in there?"

"Take him!" the people shouted.

"He's been making trouble!"

"He stinks!"

The guard sniffed at him. "I've smelled worse."

"He'll do," the other said.

As they carried Rogers to the main level, he squinted into the warmth of the sun, working its way through a low-hanging fog.

The guard ordered Rogers to walk upstairs. If he tried to run, they would surely kill him. He would have to wait for a better opportunity.

On the second level a blast of fire caught his attention as a door opened and a hideous creature emerged. Rogers had never been this close to a dragon. He felt he was looking into the face of pure evil. The eyes alone made him scamper back into the arms of the smelly guards.

"Toss him inside," the Dragoness cooed. "I know I'm not supposed to play with my food, but . . ."

As soon as he was inside, Rogers ran for the window, only to be stopped by a line of fire that would have incinerated him had he continued.

The Dragoness skulked in and closed the door, then stretched her tail to also close the window. She batted her eyes at him, sniffing. "You don't look like the rest of the rabble in the dungeon. How did you survive the flood?"

"I kept my head above water. Many are still alive, ma'am. They need your help."

"Ma'am?" the Dragoness said. "It's Your Majesty to you, knave."

Rogers ducked his head. "I'm sorry."

"Say it. Use the words."

Rogers was looking for any edge, any way to save his life, but she was not majesty to him, and he could not bring himself to say it.

She drew closer and cocked her head, examining him from head to foot. "You know I'm going to kill you for refusing to honor me."

Rogers closed his eyes and inhaled. "I do not respect those who treat the weak as you do."

"What did you say?"

Rogers merely straightened and opened his eyes, but he seemed to grow several inches taller. He locked eyes with the Dragoness, finding within himself the conviction that he served the true King and didn't have to fear this being. "You heard me. I do not revere you because you abuse your power."

A rattle formed in her throat. "I could end your life with a mere cough."

"You have no authority over me nor the power to burn away the truth."

"And what truth would that be?"

"That you fight a losing battle. That the Dragon is but a pawn in the hands of the true King."

The Dragoness chuckled and stretched herself out on the floor. She seemed to study him, moving her head this way and that. "You think the Dragon is a pawn? I assure you, he is powerful and deserves your worship as well as your fear."

"I will never worship or fear a being that can harm only my body but cannot even threaten the truth. The truth can no more be burned from us than the sky or the mountains."

The Dragoness laughed and traced a claw on the floor. "It's a pity my stomach is empty. I have to keep my strength up. It won't be long before I'll have several little ones to chase after."

A wing flap outside caught Rogers's attention, and noise from down the hall distracted the Dragoness.

"Do you really think the Dragon will allow you to live once the eggs have hatched?" he asked.

"What kind of question is that? I'm their mother."

"Have you noticed there are no other dragons in the Lowlands? He eliminates his own kind as well as us. Why would he spare you to challenge his throne?"

Rogers saw a flash of doubt in her eyes for the first time. When someone screamed downstairs and steel sounded against steel, she rose and moved to the door.

"You must make your decision," Rogers said. "You may never have another chance."

She cast a burning gaze toward him. "You offer *me* a choice? I offer you life or death, not the other way around."

"You know what I'm saying is true," Rogers said. "The Dragon will never allow another to challenge his throne, and you are more than a match for him. Revenge would make you even more fierce."

"Revenge?"

"Am I wrong? Did he spare your family? Has anyone seen them? He kept you alive only so you could bear his offspring."

More noise from downstairs. A door opening down the hall. *Crunch, crunch, crunch.*

The Dragoness's face contorted in terror—a look so horrible that Rogers knew the sound had enraged her. She flapped her wings and flew from the room.

Rogers followed, passing the still bodies of guards on the stairs and rushing toward the nursery.

There, standing beside five smashed eggs, Talea protected behind him, was the Wormling.

"You've killed my babies!" The Dragoness's voice cut the air with pain and anger.

"Your evil will not live on after you," the Wormling said.

"My children," the Dragoness whimpered. "My beautiful babies. Where have you gone? Oh, forgive me for not taking care of you." She bent to examine the nest, suddenly turning on the Wormling. "You didn't do your job. There is still one left." She pointed to Talea. "You'll pay for this. You and your friends will die like your family. And know this: I will have more children."

"My family?" Talea wailed.

The Wormling raised his sword at the Dragoness. "Greater is the creator than the created. Prepare to die."

She shot fire at the two that lit the room like a blowtorch.

Rogers retreated and grabbed a spike from a fallen guard. But as he dived toward the Dragoness, the guard caught his ankle, sending him sprawling.

The Dragoness continued her blast, turning the room into a furnace and making Rogers wonder if the Wormling or Talea could survive. He kicked free of the guard and leaped onto the Dragoness's back, plunging in the spike.

She yelped and turned, throwing Rogers off, then whirled on him and fired away again. But the flame went straight up and fizzled, and Rogers saw why. The Wormling had driven his white-hot sword deep into her heart, only the hilt showing from her chest as she thrashed and crashed to the floor atop all but one of her broken eggs.

"Is she dead?" Talea said, clearly paralyzed from fear.

The Wormling pulled the sword from the Dragoness, and her body fell limp. "She won't harm you. We would never be able to do that to the Dragon—his scales are much thicker at the chest."

"My family," Talea said. "Are they really gone?"

Rogers tried to speak, but the look on his face was evidently all she needed. "There was a flood," he said.

Talea's eyes filled and she gritted her teeth, lunging toward the last egg.

The Wormling grabbed her before she brought her weight down on it.

"You save the Dragon's offspring? I want every one of these gone!"

"I have need of it," the Wormling said.

He assured Rogers that the guards had been taken care of and that he could release the remaining captives. They staggered into the light, wet, hungry, and thirsty, their clothes in tatters and their skin peeling. Many apologized to Rogers and thanked him.

The Wormling brought food and water for all, and then they burned the palace and everything in it.

As the people slowly set out for their homes, the Wormling beckoned them to follow him. Only a few did, and one family agreed to look after Talea along the journey.

Finally, Rogers was alone with the Wormling once more.

"I wish we could have spared the Dragoness and enlisted her against the Dragon."

The Wormling shook his head. "We are at war. We cannot convince evil to change. Evil consumes everything in its path. Do not feel bad that we rid ourselves of some of it."

The Wormling helped Rogers prepare the people for their trip, then explained some of his plan as he led Rogers to Grandpa for their flight.

"Why are you keeping one of the eggs?" Rogers said.

"You will find out," the Wormling said.

Rogers was surprised to see Machree.

"No one must know of his involvement with us," the Wormling said.

Rogers nodded, but he worried whose side the bird was on.

39

Silent Scream

Clara had used her back door key and moved Connie into the boarded-up Briarwood Café. It was a good place to hide, where she could find food and water. The aging process had further attacked Connie, making her even thinner and nearly unable to swallow.

Clara dragged a table in the corner to a booth, making a long table, and used several tablecloths to keep Connie warm. Clara made sleeping quarters for herself in a booth nearby, where she could see outside through gaps in the boards tacked over the windows. She had seen police cars and ambulances since carrying Connie from the bed-and-breakfast but not much else.

Early in the morning Connie was rasping and coughing. Clara had seen shadows move past the windows, though when she peered out, she found nothing but wind in the trees and a dim streetlamp.

"Water," Connie moaned, barely loud enough to be heard.

Clara brought her a glass and lifted her head.

Connie took a few sips, then lay back on the pillow Clara had made from linens.

"How are you feeling?"

"As bad as I look," Connie said. "I've always dreamed of being a princess, but when my horse-drawn carriage arrives, it had better be a wheelchair."

Clara pushed the hair from Connie's eyes and smiled. "It's good to see you still have your sense of humor."

"With all these wrinkles, it's the only sense I have left. What about you? What are you supposed to see in this new world of your father's?"

"He didn't tell me much," Clara said. "I assume he'll tell me when I'm supposed to know. I'm still getting used to who he is and who I am. I'm not sure I want to know everything just yet."

Connie nodded weakly and took a shallow breath. "Do you think he meant for this to happen to me?"

Clara looked away. "Well, if he's truly in control, I suppose he could have prevented it. So there must be some purpose in it."

"In feeling like you're going to die? I can't imagine."

Clara fumbled in her pocket for a scrap of paper. "I wrote something from *The Book of the King* down. Listen. 'Every detail of your life is woven like a beautiful tapestry. Whether it seems good or bad, it perfectly fits into the design. Your father loves you—'"

"Shh . . ."

The doorknob turned slowly. A deep voice. Then something pressing against the door.

"Stay there, Connie."

"As if . . ."

Clara grabbed a chair and shoved it under the knob, wedging it tight.

When the next volley of pushing came, someone cursed. "We're going to have to break a window." Clara recognized the voice.

"Let me try," another said.

The door banged, cracked, and rattled, but the chair held. More cursing. "Once we're in, check the register just in case. I'll look for pies or those ice cream cakes from the freezer."

Clara took a deep breath. "Looks like company," she said in her most manly tone. "Call the cops and I'll get the gun."

Someone laughed and slammed against the door, splintering the wood and sending the chair flying.

Clara screamed and rushed to Connie, covering her.

"Gordan!" she said as he crashed halfway through, pant leg caught in the wood.

"Who is it?" someone behind him said. Clara assumed it was one of his usual lackeys.

"Clara. The pretty one with dark hair. The waitress. How're you doing?"

"What's that?" someone said outside.

"Let's get out of here!" another said.

"Guys," Gordan said, "don't leave because of a little fog. Honey, can you give me a hand over here?"

Clara shook her head as a misty white seeped in and billowed about.

Gordan coughed and struggled. "Come on. Help me!"

Before she could move, a sticklike arm shot through the opening. Several feelers extended and wrapped themselves around Gordan's chest. His eyes grew wide as they tightened, squeezing the breath from him.

Clara rushed to pull at the spiny tentacles, but they were so tight she couldn't even get her fingers underneath. Something snapped, and Gordan looked like he wanted to scream. Clara actually felt sorry for him for the first time in her life.

An object—curved and sharp and glistening—moved

through the broken door. It looked like the talon from some ancient bird. With a quick pull, Gordan disappeared into the mist. Clara heard a gurgle and something splattered on the door. Then a thump on the ground, as if someone had dropped a sack of groceries. Clara froze as a tentacle reached into the room, twitching as if sniffing.

The thing, whatever it was, moved farther in, displaying more tentacles, more feelers. When its huge head popped through the door, it looked like Karl, only bigger, stronger, and more hideous—with a smell that rivaled a pail of dirty diapers.

Clara stepped back, bumped into a table, and toppled over a chair.

The creature headed toward Connie and began removing the tablecloth.

"No!" Clara shouted, attacking, but one thrust of a small tentacle sent her flying across the room.

The monster grabbed the edge of the tablecloth and pulled it off, at first recoiling, then turning to Clara and speaking in a high-pitched, nasal voice. "I see you have done well in preserving the anointed one."

"Who are you?" Clara spat, getting up. One reach of a tentacle and she was knocked down again.

"I come in service of His Majesty, the new ruler of the Highlands and Lowlands. He requires the chosen bride of the boy prince. This, if I am not mistaken, is her wretched body."

"You're mistaken. She is not the one. I am."

The creature cocked its head. "Amazing. Willing to give your life in place of another. And for what?"

"She's not who you think. I'm the one you're looking for."

"Really?" the creature said, its tone unkind. "I shall take you both just to be safe. His Majesty will like that."

A tentacle shot from the beast's body and enveloped Clara. Another did the same with Connie, now unconscious. They flew high above the city, and Connie looked whiter than Clara had ever seen her. Clara prayed the poor girl would die rather than endure the torture that certainly awaited them.

For several days Batwing recorded, as best he could, the reports of Starbuck and Tusin and the comings and goings of the guards, workers, and officials in Dragon City. The only ones who left the walled city were the poor unfortunates saddled with carrying trash and animal dung and dumping it in a valley.

One afternoon the sky filled with flyers in a procession that looked like it had royal significance. Scythe fly-ers with their enormous sharp tails brought up the rear before a gap (which Batwing assumed was made up of invisibles) and a lone flying beast Batwing immediately recognized as RHM, the Dragon's aide.

"What is that he's carrying?" Starbuck said.

"Shall I fly up and see?" Batwing said.

Tusin harrumphed. "And alert the whole city that we're here? Out of the question. It's probably just more prisoners."

"There's one on either side," Starbuck said, scrambling higher for a better look.

"Be careful," Tusin said as rocks and pebbles rained on him. "You want to bury us under an avalanche?"

RHM flew his prisoners over the wall and into the city. A small cheer went up from inside and then died.

A few minutes later Starbuck clambered back down, again spilling rocks and dirt, and breathlessly reported, "He had two females with him. An old one and a much younger one. Dressed in strange clothes."

"Perhaps from the Highlands," Batwing said, "like the Wormling. Watcher said he wore strange clothes when he first came to the Lowlands."

"They must be pretty important for RHM himself to go after them," Tusin said.

"You saw by the procession that they must be important," Starbuck said. "But who could they be?"

"I shudder to even guess," Tusin said, gazing at the darkening sky. "I wish the Wormling would return."

That night it rained and flooded their mountainside cave, forcing them to higher ground. They slipped and slid until they reached the top of the mountain overlooking the city. Huge torches lit the massive coliseum, crammed with spectators. Vaxors cracked whips and struck humans who stretched animal skins across the arena to keep the surface dry.

"Many will die," Tusin said. "I can hear the growls of the tigren from here."

"They probably haven't been fed for weeks," Starbuck said. "I'd like to release them so they can attack those vaxors."

Batwing shifted from one foot to the other. "The Wormling told us to wait."

"But the killing will soon begin," Starbuck said. "Surely he wouldn't want us to just sit here."

A strong wind gusted from below, and a great presence loomed over the three.

Starbuck grabbed Tusin's walking stick and held it up like a sword, as if ready to fight.

As quickly as the presence came, it left, flapping into the rain. Through the darkness came footsteps, but it wasn't until Rogers spoke from behind him that Batwing knew who it was.

"It's good to see you again," Tusin said. "Are you all right?"

"Yes, but we must prepare. We don't have much time."

"That's what I told them," Starbuck muttered. "Where's the Wormling?"

"The Wormling is well," Rogers said. "He said to come up with a plan to enter the city and be ready in the morning. He says his time has come."

41

Carrying Dung

The queen of the west's back ached from the heavy load, her feet blistered beyond belief. She could barely see where she was going through the rain and her tears. She shoveled dung one day and hauled it the next, sleeping in cramped quarters beneath the coliseum where others cursed her because of her smell. Some envied her for being able to go aboveground, but none wanted her job.

The most dangerous place she gathered dung was from the cages of the tigren, where even the vaxors wouldn't enter. She had to wait until the tigren wandered into the safe section and the vaxors blocked the cages so she could run in, do her work, and get out before they pulled the lever. Plenty of people had been victims of a careless or cruel vaxor who had pulled the lever too soon just to see blood.

But as hard as her life was, it was nothing compared to the humiliation. The queen was used to being served, to sleeping in a comfortable bed, and to waking to warm slippers and fresh fruit. Now she was fortunate to get a crust of bread or a drink of brackish water.

Walking with the rough men and women assigned the same task was also difficult. She had ordered these types of people around, and now she was one of them—even taking orders from vaxors.

"Faster!" one growled as she carried her load through the gate. He lashed her back with a whip.

She screamed as the cords bit and tried to stay upright.

The path consisted of deep mud, and the people in front of her stayed in the grass, where they could get better footing. In her former life, she had had no fears beyond the occasional snake in her garden or a hangnail. Now she had nothing but fears—that the Dragon would keep his promise about her daughter, that he would consume her and her husband with fire. But her greatest fear was falling into the dung pit at the bottom of the path. Another had done this and died.

One by one the dung bearers pitched their baskets over the edge and hurried back up the hill.

Vaxors wouldn't even come close to this place. They watched from the ridge, holding their noses and laughing.

"Nice technique, Your Majesty!"

"The queen of dung!"

The valley was steep and the tossing point a sharp precipice that led down several hundred feet. A person who tumbled into the chasm would be dead before she hit the bottom, if one could believe a vaxor.

The queen was the last to the edge today and moved gingerly as she raised the pole that held two baskets on each end from her shoulders. She had become stronger here, working off some of the excess of her pampered life, but she longed for a bath and a real meal.

She tossed the first load over the edge, but when she set the empty basket on the ground, someone grabbed at her ankle and she went down hard in the mud, her momentum carrying her toward the pit. At the last instant before plunging to her death, she wrenched around and gripped a clump of grass, her feet dangling over the edge.

She screamed but no one came. The hard labor that had toned her allowed her to pull herself up a few inches and almost to safety. But suddenly the earth opened before her, and two eyes stared at her. Whoever it was tore her hands from the heavy grass and pushed her backward.

She fell into the abyss, gasping, flailing, kicking, resigned to death. But she had tumbled through the air for only a second before someone yanked her inside an area dug into the soil wall.

"It's all right now," a young man said. "You're okay. I'm sorry to give you such a fright."

She gaped, panting. "You!"

The Wormling bowed his head. "I had no idea it was you, Your Majesty. Where is your husband?"

"I don't know," she said, barely able to speak. "I can only imagine."

The Wormling held her gaze. Something about his eyes radiated confidence. Had she been wrong about him? Was there something special about this young man who had grown so strong and certain of himself?

"We don't have much time," he said. "Give me your cloak and wait here."

"Who tripped me up there?"

"A friend," Owen said.

"Some friend."

"We've watched the vaxors for several days so we could get into the city—"

"You want to get *in*?" she said.

"I have to. Now stay here until the vaxors leave." The Wormling produced a rope. "Tie this around you, and our people will pull you up when it's clear."

Without her hooded cloak she shivered in her ragged clothes. "Please find my husband and release him if you can."

Owen kept his head down and the
queen of the west's hood pulled
low as he carried the empty dung baskets through the gate, his sword and
scabbard hidden down his back.

"Wonderful recovery, Your Majesty,"
a vaxor crooned. "Thought we'd seen
the last of you."

Another laughed, but Owen just
kept moving. Once inside he was
surprised to see brightly colored apart-
ments with balconies that overlooked
stone streets. The Dragon had brought
gloom and doom to the countryside,
but these places looked at least livable.

Unfortunately they were occupied by vaxors and other follow-ers of the Dragon, and Owen knew it wouldn't be long before they made a mess of the city.

Horse-drawn carriages were plentiful, and small animals ran here and there. Judging from the number of rats, Owen figured cats were scarce.

He followed the other dung haulers as those in the streets gave way and held their noses. Little vaxors mocked them, reciting poems about the stench and throwing rotten fruit at them. Someone threw a bucket of foul-smelling liquid on them from a balcony.

The streets all ran the same direction, pointing to a white-pillared structure—the coliseum.

Owen's group was led to a side entrance that went down several flights until it became dark.

"Keep moving, vermin!" a vaxor yelled.

Down they went, through iron gates that slammed and locked behind them. In the bowels of the structure Owen could hear the roar of tigren and the clang of metal against metal. He glanced at people in cells as he passed and recog-nized a few of them. *Why are they being held?*

"Inside and stack your baskets," a vaxor shouted. "You know the drill."

They were herded farther down to yet another entrance, where they were locked away. People coughed and wheezed, collapsing from exhaustion. Many looked as if they hadn't eaten in days.

"My lady, you took a terrible fall," a man said, approaching Owen. "Are you all right?"

His hood still covering his head, Owen nodded and quickly moved to a corner, where he leaned against the wall.

But the man followed. "Sorry to bother you, Your Majesty, but I've news of your husband."

Owen recognized Dalphus, the king of the west's armor bearer.

The man's already pale face blanched at the sight of Owen, his mouth dropping. "What have you done with her?"

Owen grabbed the man and pulled him to the wall. "Keep your voice down. Your queen is free."

"But how?" Dalphus whined. "We are watched every moment."

"My friends have her," Owen said. "Now what do you know of the king of the west?"

"He is jailed with the group to be led out first tomorrow for the opening ceremonies."

"Ceremonies?"

"Celebrating the Dragon's triumph over his enemies. The vaxors say the king is to be eaten by the tigren. His wife is to be spared until she sees the blood of her daughter spilled on the Dragon's throne."

"They have captured Onora?"

"So the vaxors say. Of course, who knows if—?"

Owen turned toward the wall, whispering, "Everything is coming to pass just as it was written."

"What are you saying? This is part of some plan?"

"Exactly. And though it may seem otherwise, it's working perfectly."

"Ach! Who would come up with a plan that has the Dragon on the throne, killing the king and queen of the west and their daughter as well as the King, his wife, and his children?"

"Children?"

"I overheard a vaxor say the Dragon's right-hand man returned with not only Onora but also with Gwenolyn, the King's daughter."

"She stayed with her to the end," Owen said, tears coming. "What does he believe about the King's Son?"

Dalphus winced. "The Dragon believes he is either dead or cowers somewhere in the Highlands."

Owen drew closer to Dalphus. "Know this. The Son does not cower. Nor is he dead. And the King's plans will be completed in spite of the Dragon's plot."

"You are the Son?"

"You were there when I told the king and queen of the west my identity."

"But how can you know this?"

"The same way I know the sun will rise and dispel the darkness each morning. The way I know beyond doubt that we have all been put here for a purpose. The way I know that with each heartbeat a destiny of greatness calls, telling us we are part of a much bigger story, with a secure future."

Dalphus stared, mouth agape.

"Tell your friends to be ready to fight," Owen said. "Spread the word that the return of the Son is near. Do we have weapons of any kind?"

"Just the sticks they gave us to gather dung and the poles to carry the baskets across our shoulders."

Owen nodded. "Sharpen them."

Onora's Interview

Connie lay under a canopy on a soft bed in the corner of a huge room. A vase of flowers and a basket of fresh fruit sat beside her. The trip from the Highlands had all but taken her last breath. She had lost track of Clara and wanted to ask where she was, but the creatures that tended her were not friendly-looking and had not even spoken.

When the beast that had captured her entered, she tried to sit up, but she was light-headed and fell back.

The beast cleared his throat. "His Majesty, the king of all lands, wishes a word with you."

Both doors opened, and a creature

ducked to get through and once inside seemed to gain stature as he puffed out his chest. At once she recognized the Dragon who had tried to kill Owen and her at the B and B, the one who breathed fire and terrorized them the day Mr. Page had first left.

"My dear Onora," the Dragon purred, "how lovely you look . . . for your age."

Connie remained silent, looking the Dragon in the eye, which, she could tell by his reaction, rarely happened. The beast was used to victims cowering and whimpering and pleading for their lives.

"Did you have a nice trip from your world? I hope my friend here wasn't too rough with you."

"Why did you bring me here?"

The Dragon chuckled. "I think you know. You are needed."

"For what?"

"Why, to marry your true love, your intended. Unless, of course, your intended doesn't show up."

"I'm not stupid," Connie said, her voice as strong as she could make it. "You have no intention of seeing me—"

"I read it in the book," the Dragon said. "Lots of wonder-ful things about new worlds, blue skies, blah, blah, blah. You must be terribly excited."

"I'm terribly old."

"You are. But the effects of the minions of time can lessen.

You could still enjoy a long, productive life *if* you swear allegiance to me and my kingdom."

"Why would I do that?"

The Dragon held out his arms, talons up. "I don't know, perhaps to avoid the prospect of being cut open and having your blood anoint my throne, then being burned alive? Doesn't that sound icky to you?"

"It does."

The Dragon smiled. "I thought so."

"You're wasting your cinder-stained breath," Connie said. "Swear allegiance to you? With my dying breath I'd spit on your throne. But I don't plan to die, for the Son of the King and I are to marry, and our union will signal the end of your reign. Indeed, every word the *true* King wrote shall come to pass."

A rattle sounded in the Dragon's throat. "I should consume you right now, but I wouldn't want to disappoint your parents. I promised they'd see you expire, and I always keep my word." He turned and addressed his aide. "RHM, she believes the Son remains alive."

"Yes, Your Majesty," RHM said. "But regardless, he is of no consequence. Hiding in the Highlands or dead, it doesn't matter. The enemy has lost."

True evil is perilous if one gets too close, as it can taint the soul of even the onlooker. However, to understand true goodness and purity, we must view true wickedness. It would be much easier to turn away—and perhaps less painful—but as we have seen, easier is not always best. In fact, as *The Book of the King* states, *Nothing good is ever easy.*

The day dawned bright and clear over Dragon City. Banners unfurled, marketplaces filled, and eager vaxors and the curious made their way to the coliseum for the bloodletting of the innocents.

The crowd made haste, not simply

because they feared missing the opening ceremonies but because the Dragon had decreed that latecomers would face the same fate as the unfortunates waiting behind bars to provide the entertainment.

Beneath the floor of the arena, before the hot, cramped, nearly airless dungeons, the chief vaxor, Velvel—one of the few survivors of the attack on Yodom—strutted, pacing and staring in at the pitiful victims.

They warily looked back through lifeless eyes.

"I would flood these cages and be done with you," he said. "Only one of your kind ever had the ability to entertain His Majesty, and he is long dead.

"The tigren await with teeth sharper than my sword. Their claws are like forged iron and can rip open a man's chest and pull out his heart in one thrust. Hunger and the scent of blood fuel their desire, and they can't get enough. One could kill a cell full of you in minutes. Imagine when two are released. Then four. Then six."

Whimpers greeted Velvel and made him smile. "But the tigren are not your only enemies. The bites of the sand snakes are just as deadly, though they cause a slower death. And then there is the great croc, perhaps the most entertaining beast of all.

"The crowd would rather see you run, so do yourself a favor. Run *at* the tigren or the croc and it will be over swiftly.

If you do happen to somehow survive all these creatures, you face an even surer foe—me and my company. My trained fighters will, at the Dragon's behest, torture you before we end your miserable lives."

Velvel hesitated before a woman who pressed a child behind her. He tossed her a small vial and lowered his voice. "A single drop will end the suffering."

When Velvel left, the people argued about what to do. Some wanted to fight, using their sharpened sticks. Others fought with the weeping mother over the vial. Finally fending them off, she pulled her son close and told him to open his mouth. A single drop fell toward the child's tongue as others pressed in to watch.

At the last second, Owen blocked the drop with his hand and snatched the vial. "No one will take your lives today."

"You wasted that!" a man shouted.

"Yes, give it to us!"

"Better to die here than out there for the Dragon's amusement!"

Owen threw the vial against the wall, smashing it to bits, the liquid sizzling and smoking as it ran down the bricks.

With fire in their eyes, the crowd rushed Owen, and a single sound stopped them from tearing him limb from limb— the blow of a horn from high above. The roar of the crowd followed.

"Take courage," Owen said. "The Dragon's reign will be short-lived."

"How do you know?" someone said. "What makes you so great that you can order us?"

Others hollered their agreement, and again they rushed him.

But Owen flipped off his hood and reached down his back, drawing out the Sword of the Wormling, steel zinging against the scabbard.

The people shoved each other to get away.

Owen drove the sword into the sand. "You've heard it said: united we stand—divided we fall. Pull together and defy the Dragon."

"Stand against the beasts? You're crazy."

"When the vaxors come, carry your sharpened sticks behind you. And do not be concerned about the beasts."

"He's mad."

"A lunatic!"

The child Owen had saved stared up at him with big, round eyes. "No, he's the Wormling."

Owen smiled and knelt. "'From the mouths of children comes truth. Fulfilled and happy are those with pure hearts. You will see the truth. And you will be freed by it.'"

"Can't be," someone said. "The Wormling is dead."

"And he was much taller and stronger."

Owen chuckled. "I'd like to meet that Wormling. But he

does not exist. I am the Wormling, and despite all arrayed against us, we will be victorious today."

"If you're the Wormling, tell us something from the book."

"The book is safe, with friends."

"Oh, sure! Then tell us what it says."

Owen quickly recited difficult passages that spoke of hardship, heartbreak, loss, and failure. "All of these are part of our lives, but we are not identified by our circumstances." He pointed to a woman in dirty clothes. "Are you merely a dung carrier? a slave on the way to your death?"

The woman looked around. "I don't know what I am, sir."

Owen stepped toward her. "You are a precious creation. A noble woman. Not a slave to the Dragon—you are a daughter of the King." He turned to the others. "As are you and you—all of you."

"Then why are we here?"

"*The Book of the King* says no circumstance is wasted, that there is no experience the King cannot use to bring glory to himself. The King will use you today to prove to everyone that he is the sovereign. You are not here by chance."

Heavy footsteps approached, and Owen knew the time had come. The people crowded toward him, and those in other cells pushed to get close enough to listen. "Do not go out with fear. Let the words of the King ring in your ears. What the Dragon means for evil, the King will use for good."

45

The Games

RHM stepped into the Dragon's private box high above the arena and accepted the applause and cheers of the crowd of thousands. In the box, awaiting the arrival of the sovereign himself, sat vaxor leaders from various provinces, the honored warlord Slugspike, and several guests RHM had invited for their service in ferreting out hidden villages. Mr. Reeder sat in the back next to the brown-winged Machree.

RHM waved to the throng, and they quieted. "Friends and countrymen, welcome to Dragon City and the inaugural games created by and for our sovereign ruler!"

A thunderous cheer arose.

RHM waited for it to fade. "The horn you heard marks the end of the Dragon's decree against music. You may sing or play anything you wish, as long as the songs exalt our wonderful ruler. Today, for your pleasure, all remaining enemies of the throne will receive their just rewards!"

Drums rolled, trumpets blared, and a procession of acrobats and jugglers filed in, followed by vaxors carrying flags bearing the likeness of the Dragon.

"And now," RHM pronounced, "rise and remove your hats and welcome the sovereign of the Lowlands, the Highlands, and the unseen world—the one, the only, His Majesty, the Dragon!"

The music stopped and the crowd hushed.

A curtain parted and the Dragon strode through, head high, blasting a flame that caught three of his own flags on fire.

The crowd went wild.

"Welcome to the games." The Dragon's voice was nearly drowned out by the roar of the tigren below, so he bellowed all the louder. "And enjoy your stay in Dragon City! I have created a utopia most beings only dream of. A special surprise awaits, but for now, on with the games!"

More cheering ensued as birds were loosed. When they reached the top of the coliseum, they were attacked and slaughtered by invisible demon flyers. Their bloody remains plopped into the arena and some in the crowd, who cheered all the more and tussled for souvenir pieces.

The captives—men, women, and children of all ages—were led out in chains to waves of booing.

Despite the pomp and ceremony exalting the Dragon, RHM couldn't help but notice that the prisoners did not skulk and slink along but rather held their heads high. RHM signaled to the lead guard to crack his whip and put the prisoners on the defensive, but none cowered or begged for their lives or ran. There seemed a strange confidence about them.

⚜

Owen sat in a dark corner with his back to the wall of his cell as the others were rousted out. He kept his head down, hood over his face.

A vaxor doing a final sweep stopped. "You there! Up and out—now!"

Owen didn't move until the vaxor charged with his spear. He sprang to his feet, dodged, and seized the weapon, pulling the vaxor past him and crashing his head into the wall. The warrior lay in what appeared a peaceful repose as Owen moved down the dark corridor.

Owen had heard of the tigren from Watcher, who had described them as monstrously large and fierce. Now, as

he grabbed hold of the final gate to one's lair, he recalled
Watcher urging him on, her voice, soft and low, reminding
him of things from the book. How he missed her and longed
to see her again!

The tigren paced in its cramped space, illuminated by sunlight peeking through a metal grate above. The noise of the
crowd seemed to agitate it, and whenever the horns blew, the
creature roared with such ferocity that Owen had to cover his
ears. He knew these beasts had been starved for days, making
them ravenous.

As Owen sneaked into the cage, the tigren froze and
locked eyes with him, baring its fangs and tensing its shoulder
muscles. Suddenly it drew its ears back, and the hair rose on
its body. The cat crouched low and slowly advanced a front
paw through the smelly straw.

46
The Circle
of Tigren

The Dragon preened as the crowd
roared. They clearly wanted
blood, eager to see what he had
planned.

He raised one of his arms and drank
in the resulting silence. "I want to
thank all who have joined me here in
the royal box to view what is about to
unfold. Soon I will introduce a *very*
special guest who will bring with her
some little friends you will be excited
to meet. But first, another guest now
joins us."

A gate opened on the far side of
the arena, and two vaxors in bull-horn

headdresses nudged a man forward with their spears. His full beard peeked out from a scarf tied over his eyes, and his hands were bound with rope in front. He stumbled along barefoot.

"I know he does not look like such, but this is royalty!" the Dragon said, leading the crowd in derisive laughter. "See how low the king of the west has fallen."

The man was prodded past the line of other captives until he stood encircled by six metal grates. From below came the roaring of the tigren, their paws and claws reaching through the grates. Even the mighty vaxors retreated. They jumped and sprinted past the grates in the swirling dust, leaving the bearded man in place, unmoving.

"Ladies and gentlemen," the Dragon boomed, "I give you the last few moments of the life of the king of the west, who is no king at all. In fact, as I learned from his wife, he is a traitor, having assisted the so-called Wormling in an escape. He will now pay the ultimate price."

The crowd shouted insults between sips of fermented ale and nibbles at jargid-zots, warm meat wrapped in corn bread. "Kill him! Kill him!" they chanted. "Loose the tigren!"

The Dragon lifted his wings and called for quiet, shouting, "In my benevolence, Your Exalted Majesty, I will allow you a few last words! But please spare me any begging."

The king of the west pushed the scarf over his head until it fell on the ground, revealing blackened eyes and a swollen face. "I would not deign to seek mercy from one who does not know the meaning of the word. You are no king. You are a thief and a liar, and you and your followers will pay for your sins."

The crowd booed.

Suddenly the Dragon took flight and soared over the arena. "My, my, how bold and insolent! Dare I believe such eloquence actually comes from you, or were you coached?"

"Not everyone has to be told what to say," the king of the west said. "And if I had the chance to again help the Wormling, I would in a heartbeat."

"You have few heartbeats left," the Dragon said to his own delight and that of the crowd. "The tigren will soon be released, but they are on chains that reach only so far. There is one point at which none of them can hurt you. Find that area, and you might buy yourself a few extra seconds. But I warn you, one beast's chain is slightly longer than the others."

The Dragon returned to his royal seat and locked eyes with the king of the west. "I'm sorry you won't get to see your daughter, but life has its disappointments." He paused and yawned. "Release the tigren."

When the grates slid open, five beasts leaped out, straining at their leashes, swiping at the air, and gnashing their teeth while the crowd erupted. The king of the west stood still as one of the animals barely reached his leg with a claw and drew blood.

The crowd screamed, and the other animals went wild, lurching against their chains.

"They haven't eaten," the Dragon cooed. "See how long it takes once they get their paws on him."

"Sire," RHM said, "where is the other? Aren't there supposed to be six?"

The Dragon furrowed his brow and scanned the grounds. "Perhaps something is wrong with his cage." He motioned to a vaxor in the arena who gingerly trotted over, clearly knowing that if one of the other tigren charged him, he would be torn to pieces. The vaxor leaned over the grate, then fell in as if something had pulled him.

The crowd gasped, and with the other five tigren agitated to such a fever pitch that they jerked the chains deep into their neck fur, the sixth appeared. The crowd roared, but instead of attacking, the beast sat back on its haunches, licking its paws as if finishing a tasty meal.

"What in the world?" the Dragon said.

"Perhaps he's a vegetarian," RHM said, but when the Dragon was plainly not amused, he looked away.

Then the vaxor who had fallen through the grate appeared and approached the languid sixth tigren in the middle of the arena.

✦✦✦

But it wasn't really that vaxor. Owen, in the vaxor's head-dress, spoke soothingly to the tigren. The big cat was tall, and its muscles rippled as it finished licking its paws and turned its attention to getting the straw off its coat. When Owen reached it, the beast lay on its back and swiveled in the dust as if scratching itself.

"Playful, aren't you?" Owen whispered. "Stay right there and enjoy this."

Suddenly the other five tigren abandoned the king of the west and focused on Owen. The nearest two came closer while the other three could only roar and gnash their teeth.

The crowd, thinking one of their own was trapped in this circle of death, appeared at first dumbfounded. Soon, though, they began chanting for the kill.

Owen raised his vaxor helmet slightly to show part of his face to the king of the west. "Don't be afraid. When you see your chance, move slowly back toward the other captives. Understand?"

Two tigren ran at Owen with all their strength, their chains too long to save him. If he turned and ran, he could save himself. But he stood his ground.

♦♦♦

"Who is that vaxor?" the Dragon said, rising.

"Just an arena guard, sire," RHM said. "No one special."

"You're wrong! He has nerves of steel. Those beasts simply sit before him. One of them just licked his hand!"

Next the vaxor twirled a hand over the head of one beast, causing the tigren to stand on its hind legs and spin, as if dancing. The crowd laughed as he pointed to another, and it mimicked the first. Soon five tigren were dancing in unison as the sixth lay sunning itself.

"The king of the west is getting away!" the Dragon said. But he sat again when the vaxor pulled a gleaming sword and held it over one of the tigren.

"Where did he get that?" the Dragon said. "It doesn't look like any of ours. See how it shines!"

The vaxor brought the sword down hard on the tigren's neck, slicing through only the chain, and the beast loped away as if in search of shade. The vaxor did the same for the rest until all had been released. Some frolicked in the sand, but two seemed to stand watch for the vaxor, growling at the guards.

"I must know who he is," the Dragon said. "Command him to get those tigren back in their cages."

RHM flew down and landed at the edge of the arena. "You

there, vaxor! Return the tigren to their holding areas. The Dragon wishes a word with you."

The vaxor nodded and waved, motioning for the tigren to leave.

All six traipsed back into their cages as the crowd whistled and cheered.

♦♦♦

Owen signaled for the king of the west and the rest of the captives to join him. He looked toward the mountain where he had left Starbuck, Rogers, Tusin, and his other friends. The queen of the west should be there by now, protected by them.

"I can't thank you enough," the king of the west whispered. "How *did* you get here?"

Owen cut the bonds that held the man. "Your wife aided me."

"My wife?"

"I believe she is safe." He glanced at the others. "And you all will be as well if you do as I tell you."

"We will," a young one said.

But the group dispersed when the Dragon landed twenty yards from Owen. "Vaxor," the Dragon said, "you have a strange talent. But this is not the time or place to show it, is it?"

Owen returned his sword to its scabbard.

JERRY B. JENKINS † CHRIS FABRY

"Will you not answer me?" the Dragon said. "Where does your power come from?"

Owen leveled his eyes at the monstrosity. "True power comes only from the ultimate source, the one who creates."

"And the sword," the Dragon said, stretching his neck to see the weapon. "It is not one of ours."

The prisoners, flanked by vaxors, gathered behind Owen. There was no way out.

Owen walked to his left, causing sand to fall in one of the tigren's cages. The beast growled. "A warrior's sword is his prize," Owen said. "It was given to me by another great warrior."

"And who might that be?"

"My father."

"I see," the Dragon said, moving right and massaging his chin with a talon. "So your father was a great warrior. . . . What was his name?"

"He was a man of infinite kindness and mercy, so you would not have called him your friend."

The Dragon stopped and gritted his teeth. "A great warrior would have taught you obedience and devotion. You may show yours by finishing that man." He pointed to the king of the west. "Use that sword for something other than show."

"My sword will not shed innocent blood," Owen said.

"Innocent? *Innocent?* Insurrectionist, you mean! This man sought to usurp my authority."

"Authority belongs to only one," Owen said. "You have none."

"Take off your headdress," the Dragon sneered. "Tell me your name."

Though he did not know it when
he lived above the used-book
store in the Highlands, Owen had
waited for this moment all his life. He
had prepared for it by reading great
writers. The Dragon and those who
had exiled him there had hoped he
would lose himself in all those words.
Their plan might have worked, had it
not been for a man known as Mr. Page,
who delivered the book that changed
Owen's life forever.

Now, standing before the Dragon,
he slowly removed the headdress and
let it fall. All eyes were on him, but his
were on the enemy.

The look on the face of the Dragon

was worth everything Owen had been through, for what Owen saw emboldened him even more. In the Dragon's eyes was more than shock or disbelief or even anger—it was abject fear.

The Dragon's lips trembled as he edged back, glancing left, then right. "You," he croaked.

Owen pulled his sword again and spoke so softly that only the Dragon could hear him. "You ask my name? I am the Wormling, commissioned by the King himself to find the Son. You murdered my friends. You sent the minions of time to the Highlands to kill my bride. But now your end has come."

"You f-f-forget," the Dragon said. "You have failed to produce the Son. He is cowering somewhere or dead like his father."

"Oh no, foul one. Where the Son is, there the King is also. And I tell you this: he lives."

The Dragon's eyes grew black. "You lie!"

"I speak the truth. Your days as sovereign are over."

"Seize him!" the Dragon roared. "Release the tigren!"

Owen yelled to the tigren. They emerged and chased the vaxors from the arena.

The Dragon's throat rattled, and Owen gathered the prisoners behind him. They huddled as a blast from the Dragon's mouth hit the sword, making it glow white-hot, the flames deflected.

"Release the sand snakes!" the Dragon cried.

The people huddled even closer as the arena grounds began to move and hundreds of snakes slithered from their enclosures. Children whimpered, and men and women looked desperately for safety.

"Don't move," Owen said. With his sword he drew a wide circle around the group, and when the snakes reached the line in the sand, they raised diamond-shaped heads and showed their tongues and fangs. Owen gestured with his sword, and they slithered away, up the walls and into the stands.

The crowd stampeded, screaming and flailing at the snakes.

The Dragon shot another blast of fire at the prisoners, but again, Owen fended off the flames.

"I have an offer for you," Owen said, but the Dragon continued shooting fire.

One of the prisoners bolted and ran, and the flames engulfed the man.

"Stay behind me!" Owen told the rest.

The Dragon snarled as he moved for a better angle. "*You* have an offer for *me*? My demon flyers are here. I will see the rest of you dead."

"Listen or regret it," Owen said, dropping something onto the ground. "Your precious offspring will regret it as well. This is what is left of them. Drucilla is dead, the palace burned to the ground." He kicked a shell toward the Dragon. "This is all that remains, except for one intact egg."

The Dragon picked it up as if examining some ancient arti-fact. He sniffed and cradled it, then bellowed a painful cry of fire that pierced the sky.

Scythe flyers descended, and gusts of wind evidenced invis-ible demon flyers as well. The tigren ran for cover as all the forces of the Dragon were unleashed.

Owen knew his little ragtag army was not ready for the fight and had but one chance. "Let my friends leave and take me," he said.

"You killed Drucilla—and all my children."

"All but one."

The Dragon's red eyes were misty with what appeared to be a mix of anger and hatred. "Let them go when my whole army is assembled against you? You can't hold up that sword forever, Wormling."

Owen kicked off his shoe, revealing the scar on his heel. "I am more than the Wormling. My father is the King! I am the Son, heir to the throne and your mortal enemy. The one I sought, whom you meant to kill, and I are one and the same. My marriage will unite the worlds and everyone in them."

The Dragon's lips moved, but no words came. He stared at Owen's heel. "You?" he said finally.

Owen nodded. "Now free these and any others in your charge. You can have my life."

"No!" a child said. "You're the King's Son! You can't leave us!"

"Whom do you have but these?" Owen said.

The Dragon snapped his fingers. "Bring the queen of the west. And the others."

RHM appeared over his shoulder. "*All* the others, sire?"

"Yes," he said, calling off the air attack. "And now, Wormling, hand over your weapon."

Murmurs swept throughout the hillside where the captives had fled to join Owen's other friends. Some couldn't believe the Wormling was the Son. Others thought him crazy for not fighting. Nearly all thought they should keep moving farther from Dragon City.

"We stay here because that is what the Wormling requested," Batwing said.

"That was before he surrendered," a man said. "He proved he cannot be trusted. How does he know the Dragon won't simply come and wipe us out?"

Several spoke at once until the

king of the west hushed them. "We must stay together, of one mind." His wife huddled close and wept.

"Don't you see?" a woman said. "The Wormling didn't care for his own life. He cared for us."

"But we would have fought for him," another said. "We would have helped him defeat the Dragon and bring in his kingdom. Even if it meant our lives."

Some said they could never defeat the Dragon and his forces. Others said they should raise up a new leader. "Send an assassin to kill the Dragon, and his forces will scatter."

Someone emerged from the heavy fog that enshrouded the mountain and spoke as if he'd been listening all along. "You cannot kill the Dragon by conventional means. He can exist in the Highlands, the Lowlands, and in the heavenly realm."

"What does that mean?"

"How do you know this?"

"My name is Tusin." He sat, his cape folding over his body. "I have spent time with the Wormling—the Son. We helped him and his friend Watcher. We knew the King."

"What about the Dragon?" a man said. "How do we kill him?"

"*The Book of the King* speaks of it. The Wormling told us much about his plan but not all. One thing we know is that the Dragon has layers of scales on his chest and back that make it impossible for even the Sword of the Wormling to pierce all the way to his stony heart."

"If it's impossible to kill him, what are we—?"

"It's not impossible. I'm simply saying it will take more than a sword. The Wormling says the plan was laid out by the King in his book. We are to have faith, no matter what."

"He will be killed," someone said. "The Dragon will kill him and then come after us."

"We are not alone in this fight," Tusin said. "We have allies, even inside the Dragon's trusted circle. And reinforcements."

"From where?" the queen said.

"I don't know, but the Son promised, and I believe him."

"What of our daughter?" the king said.

Tusin pursed his lips. "The Son has a deep love for all of us but an even deeper love for her. He knew the Dragon would not release her. It's all in the book."

"What are we to do?" the queen said.

A flutter of wings passed overhead. Tusin rose and moved up the hill. "We stay here. And we prepare for battle."

As murmuring rose in the crowd again, a young girl sat crying, grieving the loss of her family.

Rogers sat beside her, and beside him was a mud-covered Starbuck, cradling the book.

49

The Council

The Dragon marched into the council room of the coliseum, and all the members applauded. These most fierce and terrible beings in the Lowlands sensed victory. The newest member, Machree, spread his wings and smiled in welcome of the Dragon.

"Where have you imprisoned the Son? We should kill him now!"

"He's your sworn enemy! Flood his cell!"

"Extinguish him with fire!"

The Dragon lifted a hand. "Guards watch every door between him and freedom. There is no escape."

"Sire, let me be the one to end his life," Slugspike said. "I will bring his body so you can burn it before the crowd at tomorrow's ceremony."

"Generous of you, Slugspike, but you see, he has not given up the whereabouts of the one offspring that still exists."

"Allow me to gain this information from him," another said. "I can do it while keeping him alive at the same time."

"In due time," the Dragon said, rising to ceremoniously hang the Sword of the Wormling on the wall. He gazed at it lovingly and scratched himself, his confidence at an all-time high. He turned. "What about you, Machree? As our newest member, what do you think we should do with our prisoner?"

Machree dipped his head. "I defer to your knowledge and wisdom, Excellency."

"I appreciate that, but I really want to hear your thoughts. We've become so ingrown. It is useful to get an outsider's perspective. Please."

"Very well. I think it best to use this situation as the ultimate proof that you are sovereign. You were going to execute the girl in front of her mother—"

"And I will yet," the Dragon said.

"Of course, sire. But her mother is gone. How much better to do this in front of the Son and see the look on the his face. . . . Would that not be priceless? He will certainly give you the location of the egg at that point."

RHM said, "We only wish we could have met the mother of your child."

The Dragon scowled. "She was useful for this task, but that is all. I do not grieve her, just the destruction of the other children."

"How can we be sure this egg exists?" Slugspike said. "Could it not be a trick?"

The Dragon rolled his eyes. "You don't understand the enemy. He is imprisoned by honesty. He swears by himself and keeps his promises to the letter, and we can exploit that. Knowing that he cannot lie, we can push him to the brink with his bride—how is she, by the way?"

"The trip took its toll," RHM said, "but she is lucid, talking only to the one brought with her."

"The Son does not know we have both his bride and his sister in custody," the Dragon said. "We truly have the upper hand now."

Velvel raised a hand. "Do we know how the Son got into the arena? Or why?"

RHM said, "Why? He believed he could kill our leader, of course. As for how, he posed as a dung carrier and slipped past *your* detail."

The vaxor flinched. "I-I'll have them punished immediately."

"Already executed," the Dragon said. "But it all worked out. Their slip dropped him into our hands."

"A thousand pardons, sire," Velvel said. "I only hope you will rely on me again."

"Perhaps you'd like to prove yourself right now."

50

Gwenolyn

Clara tended to Connie in a room high atop one of the dwellings near the coliseum. They had heard the cheering and seen the smoke and fire, but they hadn't been able to see what caused any of it. And all the better, Clara thought, for surely someone died in that arena, probably many before the evil celebration was over.

Vaxors guarded the doors as well as the balcony windows. Clara looked for any way through the ceiling in the bathroom or whether the walls were thin enough to punch through, but the structure was rock solid. The Dragon's infernal city was sturdily built.

Even now Connie's color made her

look like death itself, but something was different about her. Passing through to the Lowlands had done something to her that Clara couldn't explain.

Clara answered a knock on the door to discover a strange-looking human with a black bag. He was stooped with a scrubby beard and a crooked smile, and he peered through glasses thicker than Coke bottles. "You don't look so bad for having been stung by the minions."

"It wasn't me," Clara said. "It was her."

"That old woman? Oh, dear, this *is* going to be a challenge. Yes, indeed."

"You work for the Dragon?" Clara said.

"I work for myself," he said, toddling to Connie's bed. He took her hand and checked her pulse, and it looked as if some color came back into her skin.

"What about Owen?" Connie said.

"Who?" the man said. "Don't concern yourself with others. You have enough to concern yourself with right here."

The man pulled a candle from his bag, lit it, and held it up to Connie's eyes. He seemed to have no stethoscope or medicine, but something about him seemed familiar and kind. Quirky, no question. But sensitive to Connie. He patted her hand, and again, her skin looked younger, less wrinkled.

"Whatever you're doing, don't stop," Clara said. "She looks better already."

The man smiled. "I've done enough. At least you know she won't die. Some who are stung stay old, but you'll see her young again."

"Young again?" Clara studied the man as he packed his bag. "Did the Dragon send you? If not, how did you slip past the guards?"

"I go where I'm needed, princess. Now hold on to whatever hope you've got. Understand?"

"Hardly," Clara said.

The man put a hand on her arm, and warmth coursed through her. "Understanding is not your task, is it?"

"No."

He smiled. "Hold fast to what you know to be true, and do not let go of that."

Clara opened the door to let him out and found the vaxor guards slumped against the wall, asleep. Down the hall, at the top of the stairs, two more were fast asleep.

The man smiled and tipped his hat, then rose from his stoop and walked through the gauntlet of vaxors at full height. When he was downstairs and out of sight, Clara heard a snap, and the vaxors suddenly awoke.

51

In Chains

Owen dangled from the wall of his cell under the coliseum. He couldn't sit because the chains on his wrists were too short, and he couldn't stand upright because the chains holding his feet were too far from the wall. At first it had been uncomfortable. Now, after hours in the dark, it was excruciating. The guards had beaten him with chains, yelled insults, and spat on him. They mocked his father, saying he was no king compared to the Dragon.

Owen had been confident he had followed *The Book of the King* up to now. It had referenced the people of

Perolys Gulch and prophesied that the Dragon would try to have offspring. He also knew he was to reveal his true identity to the Dragon. That was to make the Dragon believe he had control over the Son. But Owen had not anticipated being in a dungeon without his sword, the book, or any friend to call his own.

A rat scurried toward him, whiskers twitching.

"How are you, little guy?"

The rat edged back, then raised its head. Owen studied the animal. Its eyes darted; then it turned and ran, tail dragging.

Soon a vaxor in full uniform unlocked the door and stepped inside with a torch. "Guard!" he yelled. "Bring me the manacle keys."

The guard came, keys jangling. "But, sir, we're not supposed to—"

"You've got him in an impossible position. And look at the water dripping down his back. We're moving him." He pointed to a corner where there was straw and just leg-irons.

Several guards gathered, wielding spears and swords. The lead vaxor released Owen, helped him up, steered him to the corner, applied the leg-irons, and then—to Owen's surprise— sat and chained himself to Owen's left wrist. He ordered the others to leave and lock the door.

"Thank you," Owen said. "I was losing all feeling in my legs."

"We should respect our enemies, and you are one prized prisoner. My name is Velvel. You slipped by my men, and now I'm paying the price."

"I remember you," Owen said. "You knew Daagn and served with him."

"Yes," the man said harshly. "And it was your trickery that killed him."

"I simply used the Dragon's anger against him. Besides, Daagn wanted me dead."

"I don't imagine we will come to agree on anything here tonight."

"That's where you're wrong, Velvel. We can agree we won't come to any agreement."

The vaxor shrugged and nodded. "Good point."

After several moments of silence, Owen said, "Can I ask why you follow the Dragon?"

"Sure. He compels my allegiance by his power."

"So much for the official answer. Now really. What about him makes you want to join him?"

"Because he would kill me otherwise."

"So you fear him."

"I'm not sure we should continue this."

"On my honor, I won't divulge anything you say."

Velvel seemed to study him. "Still, this conversation can go nowhere good."

"You wish to discover something about me or you wouldn't be here," Owen said. "Am I right?"

Velvel inched closer. "There *is* an intact egg, correct?"

Owen nodded knowingly. So that was it. "I did not damage it in the least. I left it in a warm place, so it should be fine. Unless, of course, some animal happens along and cracks it."

"You should tell me the location. You don't want the Dragon's wrath coming down on you if something should happen to it."

"No, there is a time for everything, and now is not the time to reveal this."

"How do you make these decisions, Wormling? How do you know what to do?"

"I listen to my father's voice. I read the words he left for me. He loves me. That's why I follow him."

"I do not know what it means to follow someone other than out of fear."

Owen was moved. "Tell me about *your* father. What was he like?"

"I don't see how that could possibly—"

"Humor me," Owen said.

The vaxor sighed. "He was huge. Brutal when dealing with your kind. He would be gone for long stretches and return covered with the blood of his enemies."

"How did he treat you?"

Velvel shrugged. "As a nuisance. I was always in his way."

"We have much in common, except for the blood of the enemies part."

"You said your father loved you."

"My real father does. But the one who raised me, the man I thought was my father, was distant and treated me like a nuisance. My real father is the true King, who does not make people follow him. He wants them to become whole."

"What do you mean by that?"

"This world is not all there is," Owen said. "There is another just as real. My father wants to unite the seen with the unseen. When these worlds are whole, everything will change. His love will be seen, and we will follow him because we love him, not because he threatens us."

The vaxor's eyes shone, firelight dancing on his face. "And what of the Dragon?"

"His defeat is sure. He will not rule this world or any other."

Velvel harrumphed. "You say that as if you really believe it. Yet here you sit in chains, with no army and all the forces of the Dragon against you."

"But I have seen the end of this war already. I have spoken with the one who wrote *The Book of the King*—"

"Tell me of this book."

Owen hesitated. "I don't know if I can trust you. In fact, I'm pretty sure I can't. Why should I?"

Velvel narrowed his eyes. "I think of myself as a fair warrior. If the Dragon asked me to kill you, I would." He lowered his voice. "But I sense something in you. And if there is a chance you could be right . . ."

"Listen carefully," Owen said.

52

The Visitor

Rogers tried to comfort Talea, but the girl could not stop crying. "Why did I care for those eggs so well," she said, "when I should have known my family was dying?"

"You couldn't know," Rogers said. "You were working to keep them alive."

A shout came from the edge of the camp. "Vaxor on horseback!"

Starbuck and Rogers left Talea to gather with the warriors. They would be hopelessly outmatched against any of the Dragon's forces, but they quickly flanked the invading rider from behind.

"Now!" Rogers said.

Starbuck threw his spear, and the

rider fell with a thud. Several men held knives at his neck as he slowly rose. The spear had only knocked him off his horse; it had not pierced his armor.

Tusin stepped forward. "Identify yourself."

"I am Velvel, chief of the vaxor forces of Dragon City, leader of the imperial guard."

"And what reason have we to let you live?" Tusin said.

Velvel glanced from face to face. "I'm looking for Starbuck."

"What do you know of Starbuck?" Tusin said. "Who sent you?"

"He who sent me said you would know who he was by the fact that I knew Starbuck's name."

Everyone grew quiet.

"How is he?" Tusin said.

"Chained, imprisoned. He has been beaten."

Rogers raised his spear. "Let's kill this one now before he alerts others."

"There are no others," Velvel said. "I've come alone."

"What do you want with me?" Starbuck said, pushing his way through the crowd.

"I was told you hold the book."

The crowd gasped and Starbuck winced. "No books are allowed in the Lowlands—you know that."

"Don't pretend you don't know I'm talking about *The Book of the King*. Your leader asked that I retrieve it."

"Don't believe him!"

"He's a liar!"

"The truth is not in him!"

"Don't trust someone who works for the Dragon!"

"Quiet," Tusin said, studying the man.

"He's luring us into a trap," Rogers said. "We let him go and he'll lead the rest of the horde here."

Tusin grabbed Velvel's chin and forced him to look him full in the face. "Your eyes have been opened, haven't they? You've heard the truth about the King."

The vaxor wrenched away. "I listened. I haven't made up my mind about what is to come."

"You're playing both sides," Starbuck said. "You'll go with the Dragon if he wins and the Son if he does. But that won't work. You have to choose."

"The book says, 'If you stand on a fence in the middle of battle, you can't help but fall,'" Rogers said. "Which side will you serve?"

Velvel looked around. "I risked my life and my career to come here. Don't accuse me of not choosing. Plus, your friend told me you would believe me if I explained what he said."

"And what was that?" Starbuck said.

"That the King's plans are coming true. No matter what happens, believe the Dragon will be defeated. But your friend has need of the book. And he must have it now."

53

The Dialogue

Early in the morning, even before the sun would begin to bathe Dragon City, the Dragon sent for his prize prisoner—the sworn archenemy and last threat to his throne.

The Dragon had not slept, pacing and plotting how to best elicit from the Wormling the whereabouts of his last egg and then dispose of him. Some had suggested he raise the boy high on a stake so the sun would bake him for days. Others said he should bury the young man alive. Still others felt he should be bound and thrown into the shallow muddy pit of the crocodile, perhaps the most ferocious and underused beast in the arena. The Dragon worried, however, that the Wormling/Son would use his power over the croc as he had the tigren.

As the Dragon waited for RHM and vaxor guards to deliver the boy—as he insisted on referring to him—he was pleased to see that his own ornate quarters were expansive and clean, with fresh fruit and juices all around. That alone should show the cursed boy the difference between his predicament and the Dragon's existence. One lived in splendor, waited on by staff eager to do his bidding (if they knew what was good for them), while the other was chained to a hulking vaxor in a dank, musty, smelly, cramped, dark dungeon.

When the Dragon finally heard footsteps in the long corridor, he took one last peek at his visage in a full-length mirror. His eyes looked droopy from lack of sleep, but he was otherwise pleased with every green scale, horn, tentacle, claw, and talon. He spread his wings and lifted his tail so that his ginormous body filled the frame. Baring his teeth and turning his head this way and that to admire them all, he wondered why humans found his kind repulsive. Why, if he had the time, he could gaze at himself all day.

When the knock came at the door, the Dragon hurried to the window and struck a reflective pose, gazing at his empire in the pink light of dawn. "Enter," he said, but when a second knock came, he realized RHM could not hear him with his back to the door. He craned his neck and bellowed, "It's open!" then returned to the view.

The Dragon stood cupping one arm and stroking his chin. Behind him he heard the clanging and scraping of vaxor armor as well as the jangling chains of the prisoner. He waited until RHM cleared his throat, then turned, as if surprised. "Oh, unchain the lad," he said. "Free both hands and feet. You are no flight risk, are you, son? We are now but business-men hammering out an agreement; are we not?"

The young man, who looked less than heroic after what had to have been a rough night for him, merely stared at the Dragon as the vaxors removed his chains. His clothes were torn, and there were marks on his face and chest. He winced when the vaxors removed his handcuffs from behind, and the Dragon knew his back had to be raw from his beating.

"Sit, sit, please! Fruit? Some juice perhaps? I'm not sure these are offered below, are they?"

It was not lost on the Dragon that the boy glanced long-ingly at the bowl of fruit, even while declining. The boy sat straight, avoiding pressing his back against the chair, as RHM and the two guards stationed themselves near the door.

The Dragon sat and took a deep breath. "Then let's chat, shall we? I'm curious why you would invade my arena and allow yourself to be taken. Is there a rational explanation, some strategic objective, or are you simply crazy?"

"I am here doing my father's business. There are things he wants me to accomplish."

"Like destroying my legacy and my children? How cruel of you and your father."

"It is not cruel to rid the world of evil. Your children would have followed in your footsteps."

"How can you know? Perhaps one may have rebelled, become the Prodigal Dragon, as it were. Maybe he would have switched sides."

"You had your chance and chose to disobey. *The Book of the King* says, 'Do not be deceived by the smooth talk of the enemy. He has conceived sin, and when it is full grown, it will bring forth death.' That is why your offspring, save one, have been eliminated."

"But if one remains, have you not gone against your father's wishes?"

"You do not understand. My father and I have the same goals. I'm simply doing what he asked. You, on the other hand, have been a liar and a killer from the beginning."

Did this boy not fear for his life, talking like that? The Dragon was glad he had resisted the urge to hold this conversation in the arena before thousands. Who knew whom the lad could sway with his persuasive speech, speaking with authority and power and a strength the Dragon had rarely seen. He was not used to people looking him in the eye, especially when

defying him and calling him names. Most who dared try that
wound up as his midnight snacks, medium well.

"Interesting," the Dragon said, collecting himself. "You wipe
out my family and call *me* a killer. How about you tell me where
the egg is and I offer you a quick and painless death?"

"I thought surely you would try to convince me I would go
free if I led you to the egg."

The Dragon chuckled. "I give you more credit. Of course
you would have seen through that. There is honor in death
but not in the manner yours will come if you do not produce
the egg. There is no honor in the way I will have you muti-
lated before everyone in the coliseum."

"The only honor I seek is watching *you* die in fulfillment of
my father's—"

"Yes, yes, the prophecies," the Dragon said, standing and
gesturing. "The foretellings of your wonderful, majestic father.
I'm so tired of that drivel. Thus this and thus that and whoso-
ever blah, blah, blah. I've seen the book and read much of it.
Does that surprise you?"

"Why should it?" the boy said. "It did not come into your
hands by accident."

The Dragon rolled his eyes. "Oh yes, the hand of the King
moved it here."

RHM stepped forward. "I took the book from him on the
island! His father had nothing to do with it!"

"Not a bird falls from the sky without his knowledge," the boy said. "Not a leaf from a tree. He knows the hearts of all and brings health to this land, where you bring only death."

"I'm glad your father knows when a bird falls," the Dragon said, waving RHM back and leaning his massive face into the boy's. "Many a bird and foe fell in that valley while you were cowering somewhere else. Even that dithering Watcher of yours."

Finally, the Dragon had hit a soft spot. The boy set his jaw and glared, balling his hands into fists.

"Go ahead," the Dragon said. "Take your best shot. I could incinerate you right now, just as my forces turned your friends into crispy critters. A shame they didn't have skolers handy or they might have enjoyed a barbecue."

RHM doubled over with laughter, and even the vaxors chuckled.

"Kill me and your offspring dies," the boy said, "rotting where it lies."

The Dragon returned to his seat across from the boy. "Enough sparring. What do you want?"

"You know what I want. You are holding my sister and the woman I am to marry."

"Are you sure? Is that so, RHM? Were they not released with the others?"

Infuriatingly, RHM did not get it. He looked confused as he stammered, "N-no, Highness, I thought you said—"

The Dragon waved him off, shaking his head. "Of course I hold them. What better bargaining chips could I have?"

"Release them and allow them safe passage to the Amoyn Valley. Then I will tell you what you want to know and you may do with me as you wish."

"The Amoyn Valley," the Dragon said, "where you reached the Lowlands through the first portal. How convenient. And speaking of the portals—didn't the book say there were four? You came, you went, and you came again. That's only three."

The boy sat silent.

"So much for your father's prophecies," the Dragon said. "If I let them go, what's to keep my flyers from eliminating them?"

"I require news of their safe escape to the Highlands before I tell you anything."

The Dragon stood and paced behind the lad, dragging his rough tail between the Wormling's back and the back of the chair.

The boy hissed and wrenched away from the scales that reopened his wounds.

"To the Highlands, eh?" the Dragon said. "That would be four portals. But I have a better idea. How about I have a hole dug and filled with the biting ants of Glennar? Then I pour honey all over your sister and your little fiancée and watch them die, bite by tiny bite. You will be provided a front row seat, of course."

"Then you'll never learn where the egg is."

"And you would be next in the ant pit. I can begin another family."

"With the last female dragon in the land buried in the ash heap of your former home? Your greed and lust for power caused you to kill off even your own kind. Even that was used by my father. You're the last of your breed. Your death will signal the end of a long reign of sin."

It was all the Dragon could do to keep from incinerating the boy on the spot. He sighed. "So we're at an impasse. If you don't tell me where the egg is, you never see your loved ones alive again."

"I'm the one you want," the boy said. "And you have me. What possible good are they to you?"

The Dragon gave a dismissive wave. "RHM, have Velvel perform his duty. He may do whatever he wishes except for killing him. As soon as he extracts the information, let me know immediately." He leaned into the boy's face once more. "Our little talk is over, but don't forget what happens if you do not tell me what I want to know."

"And don't forget what awaits you at the end of my sword."

"Your sword? Your sword! You mean that one?" He pointed to it on the wall. "It's merely a trophy now, boy. My trophy."

Velvel arrived back in Dragon City
just in time to fulfill the wishes
of the Dragon—to take the Son to the
brink of death to get information. As
he entered the dungeon, vaxors were
strapping the boy down, face-first, on
a tilted table. Instruments of torture
were laid out beside him.

"Leave us," Velvel said, picking
through the various sharpened imple-
ments and whips. When the others
had gone, he ripped the shirt from the
boy's back. "I have to make this sound
good," he whispered.

"I know. Did you find my friends?"

"I did. And you were right about the
young one. He did not trust me."

"Tell me you brought the book."

"No."

The boy's shoulders slumped. "Then I don't know what to do. Everything hinges on the book."

"I understand," the vaxor said. "But in the end they thought it too risky."

A guard passed and Velvel raised a whip. "Now tell me what I want to know!" With terrible force he lashed the Son's back, tearing his flesh anew. On the second strike, the Son yelped and blood ran.

Velvel leaned close. "Say something. Help me stop this."

The boy shook his head and yelled, "Never!"

As the Son writhed and cried out with each new torture and blow, more vaxors appeared, apparently eager for their turn at him.

But the more Velvel focused on his task, the more he came to respect the Son. Velvel had never had a victim go this long without breaking and revealing whatever information the Dragon wanted. But there was something deeper working in this lad.

Something about the Son drew Velvel, but as he flailed away, he had to admit to himself that he wasn't entirely sure what he would have done with the book if he had it. Something was going on inside him that he didn't understand. He had always been committed to the Dragon, but now a sliver of doubt had crept in. He wanted to be on the winning side and enjoy the spoils of victory, to march into the arena to the cheering crowd and exult in the Dragon's fire. But the way this boy talked, the way he recited from a book that seemed to possess him, made Velvel wonder if he was on the right side after all.

To make matters worse, as he pummeled this human, something began to pierce his heart. What the boy had said about becoming whole struck him. Was it possible that *he*, a vaxor—a brutal warrior with nothing but bloodlust coursing through his veins—could be changed in some way, himself made whole?

He put the boy on a rack that stretched his legs until they nearly broke, which caused screaming but no talking.

"You want to tell me where it is now?"

The other vaxors laughed and pointed, shouting insults.

But finally Velvel knew he had to stop. He turned to the crowd outside the cell. "Leave me alone with him. I sense he's at the breaking point." He put down the whip, released the boy from the device, and sank to his knees in the dirt. Was this nagging in his mind just the effects of bad wine and moldy cheese? Or had some strange hope been planted in his heart that, just maybe, there was more to life than killing, pillaging, gorging himself, and drinking himself into a stupor, all the while trying to please the never-satisfied Dragon?

A vaxor returned. "Let me relieve you," he said.

Velvel shook his head. "Stay out. I nearly have him talking."

"You nearly have him dead. You could bathe in his blood."

Velvel waved him off and leaned down to look into the boy's eyes. He was breathing—that was all. And suddenly, as if falling from a fence, Velvel's heart went cold. What had he been thinking? Would he give up everything the Dragon promised for words from this otherworldly lad?

He rose and rushed from the cell, locking the door and ordering that no one should enter while he was gone. He ran to the top floor like a beast ready to tear apart his prey. RHM tried to intercept him, but Velvel brushed past him and into the Dragon's quarters, only to find the imperial ruler slumbering, drooling on the great table.

"I beg your forgiveness, Your Majesty," Velvel said as the beast started and raised his head. "But I have news about the prisoner and the whereabouts of his companions."

55

A New Wormling

All the while Owen was being tortured, he set his mind on a passage from *The Book of the King: When you are called on to suffer, no matter how deep the pain, know that your love and faith are being tested. Persevere and do not give up. The ill treatment you endure will help make you complete.*

Owen awoke in agony, and though it was so dark he could not see his hand before his face, the temperature and sound told him he was in a new place. He felt for the chains and found none. By crawling through straw from one side to the other, he judged the size of this cell to be about 10 by 15 feet. He felt a solid wooden door and found a tiny opening at the bottom, apparently for food. It was also the only place he got a whiff of fresh air, and the hideously smelly place needed it.

He carefully lay on his stomach because every time he moved, his wounds opened. He could hear only the clink of armor when the vaxors changed shifts. *It must be morning*, he thought. Soon the arena would begin filling.

Thoughts are like worms, and once one strays, it can lead a person down any hole in any direction. Though Owen had gained confidence through his journeys, the path his thoughts chose was not of certainty of purpose. He was wavering. It wasn't that he didn't trust the King and his plans. Rather, Owen wondered whether he had made some mistake in judgment or had misinterpreted something his father had written in the book.

Could it really be the King's plan, his purpose, that his Son wind up in a dank cell, separated from what he needed most—the book—and most of his friends buried on a hillside? How could he even hope to fulfill the purposes of the King now?

Some will tell you that everything you need in life is deep inside and that all you have to do is mine the treasure that is you. Do not believe it. The truth is that everything you need lies outside you and is given to you. It is your job to receive it, welcome it, rejoice in it, and live it.

It is the joy of fathers, at the height of a child's frustration over some loss, to dangle something even better in front of the child.

It happened this way for Owen. While he lamented his fate and questioned his choices and let the pain of his rich wounds sink deep into his soul, the hard earth behind him began to move in a slow whirlpool. At first he feared an earthquake, but soon he heard the *munch, munch, crunch* of teeth and saw a familiar glow seeping through the surface.

His heart leaped. *Mucker!*

Owen had never been on this side of the worm's digging, having seen it only from behind. Mucker finally broke through, and his old friend crawled into the cell. To Owen's surprise, following Mucker was Starbuck, intently reading a passage from the book, as Owen had taught him. The youngster didn't seem surprised that they had reached Owen.

"It's good to see you," Starbuck said, but his face turned grave in Mucker's glow. "You're bleeding."

"I'll be all right, especially now that you're here and I have the book again."

"A vaxor named Velvel came and tried to take it, but this seemed a much better plan," Starbuck said, sitting beside him.

Owen leafed through the pages in Mucker's light. He turned to the blank ones at the back, then reached for a handful of straw. "This will do."

"For what?"

"While I was being tortured, my thoughts turned to the blank pages and their purpose came to me. I knew that if I ever saw the book again, *I* was the one who was supposed to write here. My old friend and protector Nicodemus once reminded me that the author's blood flows through my veins."

Starbuck looked bewildered.

Owen continued, "The King has given me the authority not only to read and understand the words he has written but also to write them myself."

"Where will you find pen and ink?"

Owen set the book on the floor and picked at the edge of a piece of straw. "I'll dip this in my wounds."

"Your blood," Starbuck said. "The author's blood."

For the record, let it be known that the day began with cloudless skies and a mythic dawn unparalleled in the history of the Lowlands—azure blue overhead with soft pinks and purples announcing the sun on the horizon. As it rose, the pinks deepened to crimson, warning, some would later say, of an approaching storm.

Two horns sounded the reveille, adding to the excited anticipation of the crowd as they tittered and talked among themselves about the previous day.

"The Wormling said his father was a great warrior and that he would chop the Dragon's head off."

"Impossible. The Dragon wouldn't have taken such insolence."

"He seemed scared of the little Wormling."

"Watch your tongue! You'll have every guard of the Dragon on you if you keep up with that."

"I just want to see a good fight today. There was not enough blood yesterday. I want to see this Wormling torn apart and his arms and legs thrown into the crowd."

"Think of it. An arm of the Wormling. It would fetch a hefty price in the market among collectors."

"Imagine the value of his sword! Still, I don't think the Wormling will be an easy kill."

"Which makes it all the more interesting."

By late morning the place was filled. Fights broke out under the relentless sun, and the people cheered for those even more than for the docile clowns who frolicked in the ring to the delight of the younger ones.

One wielded a wooden sword and walked around on his knees. The other wore a covering that made him appear to be the Dragon. The two ran around the arena, tripping each other and poking each other in the eyes, feigning injuries and hopping about. The crowd alternately booed or cheered, depending on which held the upper hand. Finally, the Dragon kicked the Wormling to the ground, stepped on his neck, and plunged the sword into his armpit. Such a cheer arose that those at the concessions stands feared they had missed the entrance of the actual Dragon.

But first was the procession of vaxor gladiators, the parading of the snarling tigren, and the poking of the great croc brought from a watery cage beneath the floor to cavort in a muddy pit under a walkway not far from the Dragon's box.

Banners with the Dragon's likeness were unfurled, and dancers waving brown and red streamers pranced and bowed before his image. Then came the ceremonial flyover of visible and invisible flyers.

All stood at the roar of their leader, and they looked everywhere for him. A vaxor brought a live jargid, tied squirming and struggling to the top of a pole, which he drove into the ground. The crowd stared quizzically, and then their heads shot up as one when the Dragon soared over the highest parapet and blew a huge blast of fire that came within a foot of the jargid. It writhed and twisted but could not elude the flames that inched up the pole until they engulfed the animal. The straps burned through, and the jargid plopped to the ground.

A vaxor ran from his post, stuck his spear into the animal, and hoisted it for the cheering crowd. Then he deftly ripped off some hide with his knife, sliced a chunk of meat, and gave a thumbs-up as he tasted it.

The Dragon took his place in his box and addressed the throng as if they had a choice whether to be here. "Thank you for joining me on this festive occasion. We have a perfect day to celebrate the end of the threat against our new kingdom."

Cheers and screams turned to boos when the scarred, bleeding Wormling was wheeled before them, standing strapped to a pole in a wood cart pulled by a mule. The lad's chest was bare and the marks on his back still fresh. Suddenly there appeared in the stands a cadre of vaxors passing out rocks and rotten fruit and vegetables. Immediately these rained down on the cart from all sides.

Finally the vaxors cut the Wormling down, dropping him in a heap in the middle of the arena.

The Dragon called for silence again. "This putrid excuse for a human is said to be the Son of a King!"

"He's not even a peasant!" someone yelled.

"You are the only king, O Dragon!"

The Dragon smiled and bowed. "One way to ensure the kingdom of this so-called Son does not continue is to destroy his bride-to-be."

From behind him a curtain opened and an old, wrinkled woman was pushed forward. She wore a crown of sticks and straw held together with mud. Her face was ashen, and a royal robe was draped around her shoulders. The Dragon beckoned her onto the small walkway that extended over the watery pit cut into the arena floor, but she wouldn't budge until vaxors prodded her with the butts of their spears.

✦✦✦

Owen struggled to his feet. The look on his face would have given spectators reason to believe the fight was not over, but every eye was on the ancient woman.

"Release the great croc!" the Dragon yelled, and the crowd came alive again.

The creak of metal upon metal grew from the floor, and no sooner had the door slammed open than the huge beast emerged and headed straight for the muddy pit. The old woman nearly lost her balance as the croc eyed her, snorting and growling and opening his cavernous jaws.

Owen moved toward the croc, catching the old woman's eye as if trying to communicate to her.

She looked down, trying to keep her footing with the prowling beast beneath her.

"Connie!" he called.

"Did you hear that?" the Dragon said, chuckling. "He speaks to his intended." He glared at Owen. "I hate poetic speech."

"Look at me," Owen said.

She looked up. "Owen? Is it you?"

"Oh, Owen," a spectator mimicked. "Come rescue me!"

Connie stared at her true love, trying to ignore the snarls of the croc and the stench of the vaxors. Owen was speaking, though she could not hear over the noise.

"*Jump*," he mouthed.

She shook her head and nodded at the croc, smacking his mouth, huge teeth jutting, waiting for her.

Owen's battered face shone with sincerity. "*Trust me.*"

He was calling her to act, to do the unthinkable simply because she believed in him.

"My dear," the Dragon purred, "I will spare your life if you simply denounce this brigand and announce your devotion to me."

Connie faced him. "You swore my blood would anoint your throne."

The Dragon shrugged. "And it shall. A mere prick of the finger satisfies my pledge. Anointing does not take a bucket."

She glanced down to see that Owen had moved closer to the crocodile's pit. Both Owen and the croc looked up at her, seeming to beckon. Was this a trick of the Dragon, an impostor, or truly the love of her life?

With the precision of a ballet dancer, Connie slipped to the end of the plank and turned to the Dragon. "I promise you I will never pledge you my allegiance, for your kingdom will fall.

You are not the true King. You are a liar. And I would rather die a horrible death than live in submission to you."

The Dragon belched fire at her, but she merely managed an old lady's wrinkled smile and dropped backward off the walkway.

Owen watched Connie seem to
float like a feather in the wind,
and the croc, perfectly positioned,
caught her in his massive jaws. He
then hurtled toward his den and disappeared underground, the metal grate
closing behind him.

The crowd fell silent at the sound of
watery thrashing and a scream. Then
they rose and cheered.

"His beautiful bride is no more!"
the Dragon bellowed. "We will cut the
croc open and bring out her body after
we deal with this one. Our fun has
only just begun."

An iron door in the wall opened, and

a phalanx of vaxors marched through, dragging Rogers, Tusin, the king and queen of the west, Talea, and several others.

Owen's heart fell. He had sent Starbuck back with Mucker, urging them to get as far away from Dragon City as they could.

Rogers's eyes were downcast. "Starbuck told us to flee, and most did. But we were delayed, arguing about whether we should go or stay. It's my fault."

"Didn't I tell you long ago that you would be by my side when the final battle began?"

"But you said Watcher would be here as well."

"She's here in spirit."

The Dragon announced, "Our search for the followers of this so-called Son has produced this ragged band. The others will be captured soon, but for now, let's enjoy the demise of these wretched creatures."

The tigren were released and they came running, jaws dripping, hungry eyed. But as if their chains had become too short, they stopped short of the group.

"Where is our daughter?" the queen of the west said to Owen.

Owen pointed to the metal grate a few yards away, where water splashed onto the sand.

"What!" the queen shouted. "You were supposed to protect our daughter!"

"Quiet," her husband said. "Listen to him."

The tigren were sent back into their underground cages as huge, heavily armored vaxors—some on horseback, some running—bearing swords, spears, chains, and nets charged into the arena.

The crowd went wild as if their lives depended on the outcome of this lopsided battle. The enemy rushed from at least 10 entrances, carrying their heavy weapons like toys.

"Stay together," Owen said. "We are stronger united."

"They'll kill us all," a man said. When the vaxors drew close, he ran, only to be downed by a horseman.

"Listen to him!" Talea said. "He saved my life! He can help us!"

Rogers clasped her hand and they all drew close, each holding a hand on either side.

The crowd grew deafening as the vaxors advanced, unsheathing their knives and swords.

There comes a point in every battle when a seemingly insignificant event determines the outcome. Owen had invaded the territory of the enemy and had been on the defensive. Now, with the help of *The Book of the King* and guidance he knew was straight from the heart of his father, Owen positioned himself strategically.

The Dragon believed he had his enemy trapped like a bug under glass, but it was then that a gentle breeze, hardly noticed, blew over the coliseum. No one heard the soft foot-falls of the oncoming masses. And no one, save Talea, saw the fluttering, seemingly directionless flight of a small, brown-winged creature that struggled to make its way over the very top of the coliseum. Something clanged against the stone structure, and sunlight glinted off metal.

Just the night before, Owen had written, *Some may trust in their strength, in their weaponry, in their number of soldiers, but I will trust in the love of my father, who delights in crushing the mighty by using the weak. He will defeat the enemy with the good-hearted friends he has given.*

And so, as the vaxors attacked, Owen turned and whis-pered to his friends.

58

Batwing

Batwing struggled and panted. He had never carried such a heavy thing in all his life, and with the enemy amassed below, he knew he had little chance of survival. One fiery blast from the Dragon would send him swirling to the ground.

Batwing tried to stay out of the Dragon's line of vision, but he finally swooped past the giant beast toward the Wormling. A blast set him afire and he began dropping, still holding on to the object.

"Drop it!" the Wormling yelled, then called for his sword as it sailed through the air and Batwing barreled into the ground. As Owen caught the weapon, Batwing's friends fell on him and put out the flames. Rogers cradled him and hid behind the Wormling.

††††

Owen couldn't wait to find out how Batwing had ended up with his sword. The last time he had seen it was in the Dragon's lair, proudly displayed on the wall. It felt good in his hands, like an old friend.

With the vaxors upon them, the Dragon standing at the edge of his box as if ready to fly into the conflict, and the coliseum's thousands on their feet, Owen hollered, "Now!"

His friends tossed sand at the stampeding vaxors, and many of them shrieked and grabbed their eyes. Owen flew at them with his sword, and several fell before the king of the west, Rogers, Talea, and Tusin, who quickly gathered up the fallen swords and passed them to others.

"Now, fight!" Owen shouted.

And fight they did. With the next wave of vaxors holding up their shields, Owen and the others moved in low, attacking legs, ankles, anything they could reach.

The vaxors, though seasoned warriors, panicked, backing up and running into each other.

Owen made it to the tigren cages and released one, speaking to it as if to a friend. The beast bounded out, sending vaxors running.

Those in the stands laughed at first, especially when several of the vaxors fell over each other in an attempt to escape. But when they saw the blood on the jaws of the beast, heard the Dragon's bellow, and saw yet another blast of fire, they fell silent.

Owen faced the Dragon, sticking his blood-soaked sword into the arena floor. "Your soldiers flee a tiny band of civilians?"

The Dragon sneered. "Just wait till you face one from my council."

"Why don't you come out here yourself?" Owen said. "Afraid to face us?"

"I would gladly engage and incinerate you, but I prefer you suffer a slower death. And as I promised the so-called king and queen of the west, I still must anoint my throne with their daughter's blood."

"Coward!" the king of the west yelled. "Liar! Thief!"

The crowd gasped.

"The thief among us is that flying rat," the Dragon hissed, "who stole the sword."

"I trusted you to protect our daughter, though everyone here should know that trusting you means death!" The king of the west turned his back to the Dragon and addressed the crowd. "Give your lives to the true King and his Son! Fight the Dragon!"

The Dragon's eyes reddened, and he belched a ball of flame at the king of the west.

Owen dived in front of it and blocked it with the sword. He turned to the king. "Stop wasting your breath and your words on brutes who do not understand their value."

The king nodded. "As you wish."

It was clear the crowd couldn't believe their eyes. For the second time in two days, and the only times anyone had ever seen it, someone had survived the Dragon's fire.

A hideous being appeared from behind the Dragon.

"Slugspike, kill all except the Wormling," the Dragon said. "Spare him until he tells me what I want to know."

"*Then* I can kill him?"

"No. Leave him near death so I can finish him off. Be careful. Like his father, he is crafty."

"I won't let you down, sire."

Owen knew his friends had not likely ever seen such a horrible beast. It crawled onto the arena floor, its spiny body oozing.

Vaxors in the stands chanted, "Slugspike! Slugspike!" and soon the entire coliseum rocked with the sound of the name.

Meanwhile, a vaxor had wounded one tigren, which now cowered, licking a spear wound. The vaxors were regrouping when Owen released another tigren. It emerged with a roar, and the approaching vaxors quickly retreated, giving Owen time to release two more.

However, when the snarling, roaring beasts had chased the vaxors back to the entrances, Slugspike advanced on the tigren, and the mere sight of him turned them into frightened cats.

Owen stood between his friends and Slugspike, staring him down. He turned and said, "Those spines shoot venom. Don't anyone try to run."

"It's useless trying to protect them, Wormling," Slugspike said. "Now step aside, and I'll make this as painless as possible."

"If you harm even one of them," Owen said, "your master's offspring will die."

Slugspike drew close and whispered with a hideous smile, "And what do I care about my master's offspring?"

A stream of liquid shot from him, and Owen repelled it with his sword. It bore holes in the sand, sizzling and smoking.

Slugspike faced the tigren, calling, "Here, kitty, kitty."

They scampered away.

"Don't harm them," Owen said.

"Like to give orders, do we?" Slugspike shot venom across the arena that hit the wall and ate through it. Adjusting his aim, he caught a tigren in the back, and the animal gave a piercing cry.

Owen set his jaw, adjusting his grip on the sword.

The second and third tigren went down with equally haunting howls, and then Slugspike waved the vaxors back out.

They approached at a gallop, backing the citizens toward

a wall where they endured a crescendo of taunts from the crowd.

"Kill them! Kill them!"

Rotten food and stones and fermented drinks rained down, and the crowd celebrated as the vaxor force pushed forward, leaving space for Slugspike to get through.

"Trapped, Wormling," Slugspike said. "Outnumbered. Surrounded. Give me the sword and I will dispatch your friends quickly."

Owen closed his eyes. "'. . . for it is not by strength or cunning or a man's power but by my spirit that you will overcome the evil one.'"

"Take the sword," Slugspike said, and several vaxors advanced with spears and pitchforklike weapons with three points.

As quickly as Owen subdued one vaxor, two more moved in, swinging their weapons. Owen knocked them away, and soon seven vaxors lay in their own blood.

But one slipped behind Owen and knocked the sword free. A vaxor landed on it and Owen fell back, now holding only a vaxor weapon. He called for his sword, but the vaxor's enormous body held it fast.

At that very moment, the ground began to soften and swirl. Slugspike's grimy feet swayed and tipped, and he thrust out his arms for balance. His face contorted as he began to sink.

The vaxors scrambled to get away, and the one with Owen's sword rolled away with it.

Owen, still whispering, pushed his friends back just as Slugspike was pulled under and then thrust on top of a mound of earth. With a sudden burst of rock and loamy soil, two sets of teeth sprang forth, engulfing Slugspike.

The crowd recoiled, aghast at such a monster.

Venom shot from his every inch and spine as Slugspike fought for his life. Vaxors in the stands were hit with his venom and fell onto the arena floor, writhing and squirming before lying motionless.

With a final effort, Slugspike clawed his way to the top, but the teeth of the great beast caught him. Slugspike screamed, and venom oozed through the teeth of the gigantic worm. Slugspike's hands rolled from the mouth of the beast and onto the ground near Owen, clenching and unclenching, sizzling with venom.

Tears streamed down Owen's cheeks; he knew Mucker had swallowed the poison to protect him and the others. Owen rushed to him as he plopped onto the arena floor. Stretched out here, Mucker looked regal though weary. The venom was already taking effect.

"I'm sorry," Owen said, putting a hand on his old friend's head. "I put you through so much."

Mucker's teeth were already gone, eaten away by

Slugspike's venom. He nodded weakly and turned his head. "I would give my life many times over for you, Son of the King."

Owen looked on in wonder. "You speak? All this time . . ."

"I was told not to speak to you. Your father wanted you to read his words, and now they are part of you. You have almost fulfilled them all, and I have completed my task."

Owen knelt beside his friend. "I knew you would come to help. I didn't know it would cost your life."

Owen turned to the approaching vaxors and started running at the one who held his sword. He picked up several weapons as he passed vaxor bodies, hacking and lunging as wide-eyed vaxors moved back. Clanging swords, vaxors screaming in pain, Owen's face marked with blood and sweat and grime, he finally thrust a spear into the leg of the one who had his sword. The vaxor let go momentarily and Owen yelled, "Sword!"

It flew to him, and he raced back to Mucker, hoping he could use it to heal him. But he felt a gush of flame and turned to see the Dragon standing over the charred and crackling remains of his friend.

Rage filled Owen, and it was all he could do to keep from throwing his sword at the Dragon right then. He knew that would do no good, as it would not reach the beast's heart through his mass of scales.

"Overcome with grief?" the Dragon said. "Imagine how you'll feel when *they* are engulfed." He gurgled and snorted.

Owen ran, shouting, "Now!"

The Dragon's chest puffed, he threw his head back, and Owen slid to a stop in front of his band of followers. Rogers was in front, trying to protect those behind him. Brave Rogers. Owen had known the moment he saw him that he was a warrior.

Before the fire erupted from the Dragon's throat, brown wings flapped behind the beast and a sharp beak sank into the scales on his neck. The Dragon roared, and the fire flew off course high into the stands, roasting a whole section of vaxors who screamed and died in agony.

Machree flew to Owen, who told the others to climb onto his back.

"Machree, you traitor!" the Dragon roared, blowing another blast of fire.

But Owen blocked it with the sword, then hurled the weapon at the Dragon's throat. It stuck there, giving his friends time to escape.

"Your kingdom is built on the sand of this city," Machree said as he flew up and over the booing crowd. "Only fools follow a defeated leader."

"Sword!" Owen called, and it slid from the Dragon's neck and back to him.

The Dragon clutched his bleeding throat and rasped, "Your bride and your detestable Mucker are dead, and your followers have abandoned you. And you cannot kill me, not with that puny sword."

"Your kingdom falls without a successor," Owen said. "You are nothing without your offspring."

The two turned round and round in the center of the arena, the crowd hooting in a frenzy.

Finally the Dragon spoke. "I will make you one final offer. Return the egg and *she* will live."

Velvel pushed a brown-haired girl forward.

"Clara!" Owen said.

Her hands were tied in back, and tears streamed down her cheeks. "Owen, I'm so sorry! I tried to protect Connie."

"You did well," he said, keeping an eye on the Dragon and his vaxors. "Don't give up hope."

"How sweet," the Dragon said. "Siblings conversing. No, dear, don't give up. I might even let you live long enough to see him barbecued."

The crowd cheered, but Owen's response quieted them. "Are you sure you haven't made a mistake? How do you know this isn't my bride and that you killed the wrong girl?"

The Dragon smirked, hesitating. Then, "What does it matter? One is dead and the other soon will be."

Someone in the box jumped up and hurtled toward Velvel,

knocking him down and, with one slice of her bonds, freeing Clara. *Mr. Reeder!*

He hauled Clara toward an exit, but several vaxors intercepted them.

"A valiant attempt, you sniveling turncoat," the Dragon said. "I believed you when you said you could draw out the Wormling, but I didn't think you planned to defend him."

"You lied to me from the beginning," Mr. Reeder said. "To me *and* my wife."

"My, my," the Dragon said. "Such bravado in the face of death."

As the Dragon gurgled, preparing to release his fire, Owen put his sword down. "Release them and I'll take you to the egg."

The Dragon turned, his tail slithering in the sand. "Take me?"

"Just you and me," Owen said. "No invisible flyers. No vaxor guards. Just the two of us."

"And if there is no egg?" the Dragon said.

"Then you can kill me. I assure you, upon my word and the memory of my father, it is there."

The Dragon thought a moment. "Give me your word that you will not attack me with that sword as we fly."

"You have my word."

"Release them!" the Dragon said.

59

The Egg

The Dragon cackled as he carried Owen over the throng of cheering worshippers. "Stay and await my return!" he shouted. "I shall bring your next ruler with me!"

Having the King's Son so close gave the Dragon secret glee. How fitting that they were together now at the pinnacle of the Dragon's rule. He had conquered the enemy, scattering everyone except the Son, and would soon have control of the Highlands. In fact, his very own son or daughter could rule the Highlands when old enough. Perfect.

No one need see the Dragon kill this human—once he knew the egg's

location, he could merely tip the Wormling from his back and
let him fall. Then he would display the body in the arena,
slice open the croc, and put the body of the girl next to him.

Soon he would teach his own offspring to belch fire. He
or she could ride on the Dragon's back. His son or daughter
would rule the kingdom with fire and eradicate every enemy.

"Fly east," the boy said, his teeth chattering in the frigid air
at that altitude.

Dark clouds appeared on the horizon, and lightning
flashed. *Perfect weather for a death*, the Dragon thought.

When they neared what was left of the White Mountain,
the lad told the Dragon to fly lower. He felt the Wormling
lean and look down. *He wants to see his friends one last time.*

"Turn here," he said.

"Not to the White Mountain?" the Dragon said.

The boy did not answer.

The Dragon rose to where it was even colder. He had no
temperature issues, with his many layers of scales. The only
place on his body that had fewer were his legs, where the boy
had sliced him in the castle long ago. Lightning flashed again,
and the Dragon flew through wind pockets that bounced
them about.

The boy struggled to hang on and soon called out, "Land
over there. I need a minute."

"We must reach the egg as quickly as possible," the Dragon said. "My crowd awaits—"

"Now," the boy said, "in that cave, out of the weather, or I'll spill the contents of my stomach on your back."

Soon they were down and the lad was inside, retching and coughing.

The Dragon shook his head, rolled his eyes, and peered into the cave. Familiar. Something about this reminded him . . . that was it, the hole in the wall. This was the location of one portal. And there, before the opening the Wormling had no doubt breached, was a linen cloth that bore Drucilla's family crest. It covered something round and large, and as the Dragon reached for it, he heard a voice.

"Now you see I was telling the truth," the boy said. There was a zing of metal upon metal. "Your offspring is nearly ready to hatch."

The Dragon pulled off the cloth and gazed admiringly at the egg, all veiny and thick. "Yes," he hissed. "It could be with us at any moment." He was so enamored of the egg that he almost missed the buzzing. He had heard that sound before in the castle. RHM had been there.

"My father gave me the power to rule the animal kingdom," the boy said. "Two of your flyers learned to follow my every command. Those tigren obeyed me because they know my father."

The Dragon looked around, trying to determine the origin of the sound. "You can't order me about!"

"You are not of the animal kingdom. You are pure evil, and that is why you must be killed as well as your offspring."

The Dragon smiled warily. "And how do you plan to do that? You have no army. You have just one weapon, and it cannot penetrate my—"

"I need only the words of the King."

"Words, words, words. I prefer action."

"Very well," the boy said. "Then hear these words of action."

The Dragon prepared to blast fire, but before he could, the boy shouted, "Attack!"

The force of his voice surprised the Dragon. The buzzing increased, and when a dark beast flew out of the tunnel left by the Mucker, the Dragon belched fire too late. The nestor had already flown behind him and sunk his stinger into the flesh behind the Dragon's head.

†††

As the Dragon belched flames wildly about the cave, Owen raised his sword high and moved toward the egg, careful to stay away from the Dragon's deadly, thrashing tail.

The Dragon crashed his head against the back of the cave, and the nestor fell. The Dragon, rage in his eyes and the nestor's venom coursing through him, blasted a furious stream of fire that Owen had to block with his sword. Some of the flames diverted to the egg and charred it.

"Get away!" the Dragon roared, lunging at Owen but falling.

Owen was able to get beyond the reach of his razorlike talons, but when the Dragon swiped at him again, his claw sent the weapon flying. Owen scrambled back and called for it, but as it came he saw the Dragon bent over the egg, holding it in his reptilian arms.

Owen couldn't let the Dragon get away, so he rammed his sword through his tail and into the earth, pinning him and causing him to emit an unearthly howl. He blasted fire again, but Owen remained behind the sword, untouched.

The nestor rose from the floor and lodged itself in the Dragon's chest, burrowing through the scales. Already the Dragon was turning gray, and try as he might, he couldn't pull the sword out.

Suddenly the Dragon pivoted, his tail still pinned to the floor, and extended his body as far toward the cave entrance as it would go. He then heaved the egg so high into the sky that it became a tiny speck before disappearing into the distance.

"You killed your own offspring," Owen said.

"Perhaps," the Dragon rasped. "At least you will not have

the satisfaction. And your pain will be even greater than mine. You will never marry the one your father chose."

"Wrong," Owen said. "The croc you captured is a friend of mine named Rotag."

"But he devoured her! I watched him!"

"She was unharmed," Owen said. "Even now we prepare for the ceremony my father envisioned long ago. And there is nothing you can do to stop it."

With a mighty lunge, the Dragon pulled free, leaving half his tail in the cave. He flew lopsided and weaving, the nestor buzzing around him.

Owen readied himself to fling the sword at the Dragon's chest, where the nestor had thinned out his scales, but he held up as the Dragon escaped.

Wings flapped below the entrance, and a brown bird rose. "You didn't kill him?" Machree said.

"Soon," Owen said. "Let's get back to the coliseum."

60

Possibility

RHM had ordered the clowns back to the center of the arena, but the vaxors in the stands grew restless, watching the skies for any sign of their leader. Velvel asked to speak with him, and RHM moved back into the corridor.

"We must face the possibility of our leader not returning," Velvel said.

"What?" RHM said, aghast. "A mere boy against a dragon? He cannot win."

"There is a strength in him I have never seen," Velvel said. "In the face of defeat, he remained sure of his father's power and eventual victory." He drew closer, looking around as if to make sure he wasn't heard. "He told me his father still lives."

"Impossible!" RHM said. "We had reports. This cloaked figure—if it truly was the enemy of our leader—was thrown down by the entire minion horde. He could not have survived."

"Do you have his body?" the vaxor said.

"No, but he could never survive. . . ."

"You thought the Wormling could not survive the Dragon's fire in the White Mountain."

RHM eyed Velvel suspiciously. "Do I detect a weakening in your allegiance to our king?"

The vaxor shook his head. "No, but I admit the boy nearly swayed me. He speaks with strong conviction and purpose. I can see how people would be drawn to him."

RHM pressed a tentacle into Velvel's chest. "If the Dragon does not return, I will be king. I will show this pip-squeak that he cannot thwart our plans. And I expect your complete devotion."

"You will have it, sir."

"Now, what else did he tell you?"

"That the Dragon would be weakened before returning for the final battle. And that the Wormling's army would march on Dragon City and—"

"His *army!* His *army?*" RHM laughed. "He has no army! They are either dead or on the run. He is deluded." He grabbed Velvel and pulled him close. "No more talk of this utter fantasy. Kill the croc and bring me the old woman's remains."

Clara's Discovery

Enjoy your freedom," an ugly vaxor said. "While it lasts." He threw Clara and Mr. Reeder to the ground outside the city.

Mr. Reeder helped her up. She was unsure where to go, knowing the vaxors could return soon to hunt them down and drag them back to the coliseum.

"I'm sorry for my part in your troubles," Mr. Reeder said. "I positioned myself in the Dragon's council so I could do some good."

"My father will be pleased. Thank you for trying," Clara said. "Should we head for those trees or down this gully into the stream?"

"Let me see," Mr. Reeder said.

Just then a man in a dark suit approached.

Clara clutched Mr. Reeder's arm, regretting that they had not acted more quickly. But when she saw the man's face, she realized it was not some vaxor dressed as a human but was actually someone she recognized. "It's the kind doctor who attended to Connie. Hello, sir!"

The man wiped mud from her face. "Are you all right?"

"I'm fine," she said, but emotion overcame her. "But Connie is—"

He put an arm around her. "Don't worry, child. Things are better than they seem."

The man nodded at Mr. Reeder, and Clara saw a look of amazement come over him.

"What do you mean, better?" Clara said. "Connie is dead. Owen flew away with the Dragon—who knows whether he's still alive? I'm in a world I've never known among beings I've never seen, and the only one who can help us—"

"Is with you now." The man took off his hat and gray hair flowed.

Clara stared, breathless. "Father?" she said, her eyes filling.

"Things are not always as they seem, my dear." He held her tight. "You have been brave throughout this ordeal. I'm so proud of you. There is much you could not have understood."

"Just being with you now is enough. I don't need to know everything."

He beamed. "But you shall, my child. It will be my pleasure to make everything known to you. Now we must hurry. The next chapter is about to be written."

The Dragon felt strength ebbing from him as he flew, his chopped tail bleeding and clotting, his throat and neck and chest oozing to scabs, his mind reeling. *So this is what it feels like to be stung by the minions of time.*

He scraped the nestor off by brushing heavily into the branches of a tree, then blasted it with fire. Then came the frantic search for the egg. Defeating the enemy and extending his legacy had obsessed him ever since he had read that infernal *Book of the King*. He overflew every bit of land where the egg could have landed, darting between lightning bolts until he came to the shores of a shining lake. *I couldn't have thrown it this far.*

He headed back to the coliseum, each wing flap reminding him how fast he was fading. His breath came in rasping gasps. When at last the stadium came into view, a roar of the assembled greeted him, and he saw a stream of warriors headed straight for Dragon City. But from where?

He landed in the middle of the arena and tried to catch his breath. RHM was there, looking concerned. The assembled vaxors had cheered him, but now they pointed and whispered.

"Where is your offspring?"

"Did you kill the Wormling?"

"No time to explain," the Dragon said. "An army approaches. We must engage and destroy them!"

"For the Dragon!" the vaxors shouted, emptying the stands and lining up for weapons.

"Now, RHM," the Dragon said, "I want that croc's belly ripped open and the old woman brought to me."

"About that, sire . . ."

"What?"

"I anticipated your request and sent guards to retrieve it. But they found a hole had been dug in his holding area and the pen was empty."

The Dragon nearly collapsed. "Not another of his loyalists!

I don't believe this!" He let out a roar, but it was weak, like an old man coughing.

RHM sidled close. "Why don't you relax at the castle and let us defeat this army? Whoever it is, we will kill them in your name."

The Dragon turned toward the oncoming storm. "No. I must meet them myself. I will see this to the end."

Over the plains of Raba in the shadow of Mount Ufel, Owen flew on Machree's back. Dragon City rose in the distance, and through dark clouds he saw the horde of vaxors streaming from the city.

"This will be a bloody battle, you know," Machree said.

"It doesn't have to be," Owen said. "Any who desire to can choose to follow the King."

"I guess I know that as well as anyone," Machree said.

The army of the Son appeared on the horizon, a mass of white-robed

warriors carrying weapons made from sticks and branches.
Owen and Machree landed and found their friends. Tusin,
the singed Batwing, Rogers, Talea, and the rest stood open-
mouthed as the vaxor force approached. Rotag slithered
alongside Connie, who was just as aged as before but seemed
to have more energy. Owen saw a light in her eyes that hadn't
been there before.

"Where's Clara?" Owen said.

No one had seen her. Batwing offered to search for her,
but Machree insisted he would so the little creature could
recuperate.

Rotag approached Owen. "Your Majesty, it is an honor to
serve you."

"The honor is mine. Thank you for taking care of Connie
and for allowing yourself to be caged."

"Who are all these people?" Connie said.

"Freed captives," Starbuck said, handing Owen *The Book of
the King.* "There's probably something in there about freeing
the captives, right?"

Owen smiled. "Yes, there is much about it, in fact."

"How are you?" Starbuck said. "And what happened with
the Dragon? I'm dying to hear everything!"

"I'm well," Owen said. "And I will tell you all in due
time. There will be seasons for stories, but now is not one
of them."

Connie took Owen's arm. "I fear for your sister. She was so kind to me. I could not have survived without her."

"Machree will find her."

"How did you know he would be loyal to the King?" Tusin said. "We always considered him a traitor."

"The King's love covers many indiscretions," Owen said. "Machree just needed encouragement."

"What is that *smell*?" Talea said. "It reminds me of the oil used to start fires at Drucilla's palace."

Owen nodded. "You will see shortly."

✦

Velvel led the army of the Dragon, but his heart was torn. His time with the Son had changed him. He had turned back to the Dragon but remained unable to still his anxious heart about the decision. Something about the words the Son spoke . . . something about the way he invited him into his kingdom . . .

Velvel knew the Dragon well enough to realize that the whole idea of ruling the Highlands, the Lowlands, and the heavenly realm had been born from the Dragon's jealousy. The true King had once reigned with a power never achieved by the Dragon. All the Dragon could do was kill and destroy and force his subjects to do his will.

But this King and his Son drew subjects with their compassion and care. They did not force obedience. They did not cajole or bribe. They simply compelled followers by their wisdom and love.

Velvel thought about this as he led the vaxor army toward the plains of Raba and some sort of massive white fighting force approaching in the distance. It was no match for the vaxors, of course, but still a multitude to contend with. Velvel figured it might cost him a thousand men to wipe out the opposition.

He shook his head, trying to rid the thoughts from his mind, but they kept coming, kept assaulting him—the words of the Son, his silence as he was beaten, his caring words, his desire to bring Velvel into the King's army. . . .

He held up an arm and the soldiers stopped at a knoll. Cremul, another commander, rode up sneering, frothing at the mouth, ready for battle. He was bloodthirsty and enjoyed killing and watching his enemies struggle and die. The vaxors wore blood as a badge, and they believed the more they spilled, the more they were worth in the Dragon's sight.

This is all our life consists of, Velvel thought. *We kill and destroy in the name of the Dragon and enjoy the spoils, but for what? To wake up another day to another battle? And once we have killed every foe in the Lowlands and we move to the Highlands and do the same, what will keep us from turning on our own?*

"We are ready to attack," Cremul said.

Velvel dismounted and knelt, scooping dirt and sniffing it. What was that smell? Why did the dirt appear wet when it hadn't rained here?

"Sir, we are ready—"

"I heard you," Velvel said. "Wait here for the Dragon. He will lead us."

"We could have this battle won before he even arrives. Imagine how he would reward us."

Velvel glanced at the vaxor, whose face was twisted in anger. He looked as if he wanted to kill anyone—even Velvel. *Is that how I look?* "We wait for the Dragon."

64

The King

Pointing the way, the King led Clara and Mr. Reeder to the Son. Then he sat on the bank of a newly formed lake, looking out over the rippling surface. It had been created when the King, by his own plan and action, had fallen through the pockets of flammable liquid the Dragon had been trying to mine. The stench was strong.

The King sat there, content in knowing that he had planted a desire in men and women to be whole, to long for true completeness. When drawn away by the evil one or even their own petty wishes, they had become fragmented and were like sheep without anyone to guide them.

All this had to happen—all this wandering, searching
for peace and happiness, settling for tidbits the world or the
Dragon offered but somehow knowing there had to be more.

*To truly drink of a pure stream and enjoy, a man must first be
thirsty*, the King had written long ago.

One prophecy remained unfulfilled, and that would signal
not the end but a new beginning. The years the people had
spent suffering under the ravages of the Dragon would be like
the burning of a plant bed. The fire kills and destroys until
new life can take over and grow.

The King rested his hands on his knees and watched
the approaching storm. Dark clouds roiled, signaling evil
approaching. But then, his Son was up to the task. And so
were his Son's friends.

65

Attack

The Dragon soared to the front lines and commanded the vaxors to advance. He applauded Velvel for not leaving without him. "Your faith in me never wavers."

The white-clad individuals on the plains looked like some society for the prevention of color, and the Dragon knew his clowns would have a field day with this back at the coliseum. With hope deep in his heart that he could still find the egg, the Dragon imagined the fun he would have reliving this battle with his little one. How they would laugh about the army in white that fell like clipped grass.

The vaxors stopped at a ledge overlooking the valley.

Strange, the Dragon thought. *I don't remember a lake here.*

As he was about to call for the sounding of the battle horn, a figure in a white robe took a stand in the middle of the field. He looked regal, as if he owned this place.

Curious, the Dragon let his hand fall and told RHM to calm the troops. "I want to see the face of this rebel."

The Dragon lumbered into the air and made a wide circle, surveying the white army. He came to rest near the regal figure and folded his wings behind him. A few scales fell from his chest, and he scraped them away with a talon.

"Take that silly robe off, boy, and talk to me like a man," the Dragon said. "I don't know where you got these troops, but you have no chance against my army."

The white-robed figure did not move.

"All right, I have a proposition for you," the Dragon said. "Surrender to me, and I will allow the others to leave in peace until a mutually agreeable time when I will demand their allegiance. Your sacrifice will allow them to live, and you'll be a heroic martyr. That's part of the teaching of your little book, is it not? Giving oneself for his fellow man?"

The figure remained still.

The Dragon exploded, "Look at me when I talk to you, boy!"

"Looking for me?" the Son said, stepping out from the soldiers arrayed on the hill. "If so, I decline your offer."

The Dragon lowered his head, trying to see inside the hood of the robed figure. But the Son raised his voice and addressed the vaxors marshaled across from his army. "My father has made a way for you to join his kingdom, to leave the dead end that is the Dragon. Simply bow to him, confess that he is the true King and that you will love and serve him from this day forward, and you will live. If you choose to fight, you will die."

The vaxors responded with uproarious laughter. They clanged their swords against their shields, and the clatter echoed through the valley.

The Dragon reached to lift the hood from the face before him.

"Your reign is over," the Queen said, her skin perfectly smooth, with not even a hint of the disease she had contracted from the banished untouchables.

Those behind her removed their hoods as well, showing themselves equally healthy.

The Dragon recoiled. "From Perolys Gulch? They are unclean!"

"No longer," the Son said. "They have been cleansed. They fight for the true King now."

"How dare you release my prisoners!" the Dragon spat.

"How dare you imprison us!" the Queen said.

The Dragon stepped back, suddenly timid. "I did allow you to live, my lady."

337

"Dragon!" a voice, like the sound of many waters, shouted from below.

The vaxors' horses fell to their knees, pitching their mounts to the ground. Everyone in white fell to their knees, even the Son and the Queen.

"You," the Dragon muttered, taking flight to the side of the lake. "I took care of you long ago."

"So you thought," the King said. "But merely believing something does not make it true."

"I saw you burn on that hill in the Highlands!"

"You saw my Son do the same, yet he stands before you. Along with those you banished to sickness and death."

"You are not as powerful as you think," the Dragon said, voice grating, teeth clenched.

"I am as powerful as a child's faith," the King said. "My strength is manifest in the weakness of those who follow me. And they shall be rewarded."

The Dragon rose and flew behind the King so everyone could witness his end. "You will no longer hound me like some vermin, no longer hold dominion over any part of my kingdom."

"You are right," the King whispered, "as my kingdom is yours no longer."

Those with a pure heart are strongest in the King's world, and it was to one of these that Owen handed over his sword.

Starbuck looked shocked but took the weapon.

"I told your father that he would sing after the final battle," Owen said. "Do you believe this?"

"I want to believe."

Owen handed him his sword. "Take it."

"I am not worthy," Starbuck said.

"Just be ready to hand it to me at the appointed time. All the while I've carried it, even in training with Mordecai, I thought it was meant for battle. As it turns out, it can be used for many things—fighting, deflecting, healing. But its main purpose stands there." Owen pointed.

Starbuck scrunched his face. "The Dragon? But how can it penetrate all those scales?"

"I will aim it straight and true, and you'll see."

Starbuck moved a few feet away and held the sword out, admiring its shining silver. "If we kill the Dragon, we still have to defeat the army amassed against us."

"The battle is the King's," Owen said. "And he will see it through."

†††

The King stepped forward as the Dragon rattled a supply of fire in his throat. "I warn you, Dragon. Do not attempt to incinerate me."

"You have no place to hide," the Dragon said, sneering. "No secret chamber to escape to."

"Bow your knee to the true King or you will surely die."

"Never!" the Dragon roared, and as he reared back to blast the King, the Sword of the Wormling flew right at him. Just as the Dragon leaned to release his molten fire, the sword struck his chest and penetrated layer upon layer of brittle scales.

The darkened heart of the wheezing old beast beat furiously until the sword pierced it, spilling blood into the chest cavity like a flood. The crippled muscle undulated and pulsed around the sword, striving to pull itself back into rhythm. Somehow the Dragon's body seemed energized by this. Perhaps it was adrenaline or the twisted thinking of a being so malevolent that made him rather have an object pierce his heart than be forced to bend his knee to the true King.

Suddenly a smile came over the face of this tyrant, and the scales on his chest seemed to stitch themselves back together and turn a lifelike color again. Little did he know that the same sword that pierced him also had the power to heal but only to preserve him long enough for the King's purposes.

"Now you will feel my wrath," the Dragon said.

⦙⦙⦙

"Everyone down!" Owen yelled. "Worship the true King!"

The white-robed army fell at once.

The vaxors had begun to charge, led by Velvel. Owen pleaded with his eyes and waved at the ground, signaling for him to fall on his knees, but the vaxor's hard countenance showed the same bloodlust as the others.

Talea whimpered, her face ashen, as the horde bore down on them with sharpened axes, swords, and all manner of other deadly weapons. From the air came scythe flyers and, from the looks of the clouds, invisibles ready to pounce.

"Do not take your eyes off the King," Owen said. "He is the one who gains the victory."

The King loomed, a majestic figure with arms spread before the Dragon.

᚛

The Dragon shot his fire across the edge of the lake at the King and the white-robed army. But he had never blasted so much heat and flame in his life, for at the first spark from his mouth, the lake rose and exploded. When the fire fell, the entire world seemed afire around them.

The King, arms still outstretched, seemed to guide the fire over his subjects and toward the oncoming horde. Those who had fallen on their faces were saved, but those bearing down on them were engulfed. Vaxors and their weapons melted where they stood.

"No," the Dragon whispered. Then he shouted over the massacre of his mighty army, "No!"

All who had thrown things, who had laughed at the spectacle in the arena, who had pledged their allegiance to the Dragon, who had killed the innocent and treated people like objects, lay smoldering. The invisible flyers were suddenly as visible as the scythe flyers, as every beast of the air committed to the Dragon fell burning to the ground.

Without so much as a whimper, the Dragon's forces had

been there one second and gone the next. The only thing
left was their ashes, and those blew away with the wind.

Tears came to the Dragon's eyes, not because of any
compassion for his forces but because he himself had
ignored the King's warning and wiped out everything he
had worked to accomplish. He wept for himself and the
end of his dream.

Looking at the King, who should have melted away but
now shone like gold, the Dragon sneered.

The King lifted a hand, signaling his followers to rise.
"Son," he called, "arise and retrieve your weapon."

As if changed into the image and likeness of his father,
the Son stood tall on the knoll, his garments glowing as well.
No longer a boy, the man was eerily framed by sunlight that
streamed through the dark clouds. Suddenly the sky brightened and clouds vanished, the sun now brilliantly covering
the land.

"I hate the sun," the Dragon muttered. "I hate the Son."

The Son shouted, "Sword!"

From deep inside the Dragon came a creaking and squeak-
ing as his chest bulged. Breaking through the scales, the sword
flew out, leaving a cross-shaped hole.

The old beast reached and felt blood pouring from the
wound. He set his jaw, and though he fought to stay upright,
he teetered and dropped to his knees before the King. And

with a final rush of air and smoke from his lips, the Dragon's head crashed down on a rock.

The King turned, his face and beard pure white, and smiled. "My friends, the battle is over. It is time for a wedding!"

Dragon City was changed with the
blast of fire and now gleamed
in the sunlight. The King and Queen
welcomed everyone who wished to
participate in the wedding. The coliseum was transformed from a house of
blood and death to a chamber of love
and happiness and hope. It was here
that all came to witness a new union
of the Son and his bride. It was everything *The Book of the King* had said it
would be and more.

Owen stood before his true father
and mother with Starbuck and Rogers
as his best men. Connie, still stricken

with age and wrinkles and fatigue, stood next to Clara as Owen pledged his life for his wife and to honor and protect and provide for her in every way.

Connie, now known as Onora to the rest of the kingdom (but always Connie to Owen), pledged to love and honor and cherish her husband, though Owen could see a hint of sadness in her eyes.

"What is it?" Owen whispered.

"How could you love me? I am still an old woman."

Owen smiled. "We have been destined for each other from the beginning. My love and the father's love can change anything the minions have done."

"But how?" Connie said.

"Watch," Owen said. "And listen."

"I now pronounce you man and wife," the King said. "My Son, you may kiss your bride."

When their lips touched, it was as if everything in the world changed. A rumble began in the distance as light and fog mixed with sparkling stars. But it was not magic. It was the power of the King to accomplish what he had purposed.

From the floor of the arena came sounds so wondrous and beautiful that the people held their breath. It was something they had not heard in such a long time, and the voice was that of Erol. Only it was coming from the mouth of a boy Owen had known in the Highlands—a musical lad named Rollie Cumis.

While the two kissed—and we know this seems like a long time to kiss and not breathe, but trust us, these things happened quickly—one by one, like people standing before mirrors, every person with a counterpart in the other world united with themselves. Mrs. Rothem became the Queen; Humphrey rose and became Petrov. Mordecai and Stanley Drones were one, and then Mordecai/Stanley embraced Qwamay/Gordan. Mr. Reeder and his wife became Drushka's husband and Drushka. Then Mr. Reeder scooped up the young blond boy below him and held him tightly, completing the promise made by the King. The Scribe rose before them and merged with Jim Videl, the editor of the student newspaper back at Owen's high school. The king and queen of the west, Connie's real parents, beamed at their daughter in her flowing white gown. All around Owen and Connie were people and beings they had known, merging and becoming one—Rogers, Starbuck, Burden, and others. Owen's sister, Clara, merged with Machree, the brown-winged bird.

As Owen pulled back from Connie, their kiss complete, he could see Watcher's eyes in his true love. And her skin was smooth and soft now, the years gone.

Owen turned to his father to ask about Clara—how she could be from the Lowlands and be united with another creature from here. But his father smiled, knowing the question was coming.

"Mysterious are the ways of the King, my Son. Your sister

347

will one day be a queen herself, and the heart of Machree, once clouded by treachery, will send her soaring."

The song of Erol (from Rollie) rose among the people, first praising the Son and his bride, then praising the King, and finally singing the song of the defeat of the Dragon. Everyone danced and sang and feasted and told stories until the stars filled the heavens.

Owen and Connie walked among the people, greeting and thanking them for joining the celebration.

"No, thank you," Connor said. "I had no idea back then that . . ."

Owen pulled him close. "The King had the idea. You were part of the plan."

Bardig slapped Owen on the back and laughed. "The Wormling *is* the Son. I would never have believed it after meeting you on that mountain."

◆◆◆

A wind blew from the north, and the King slipped away. Near the rotting carcass of the Dragon several figures stood, seen only by the King. Nicodemus, the invisible charged with watching Owen, was there. He had been restored with the joining of the Highlands and the Lowlands, and the mountains that were laid low were in place again.

"We didn't know, Your Majesty," Nicodemus said. "We couldn't conceive of such a wonderful plan." He looked toward the city. "Such harmony."

"They need nothing but the Son," the King said, "and I have given them everything in the Son. And there shall be no end to his reign."

⧉

When the time of celebration was over, Owen took Connie to a spot along the hillside above the city and showed her where their home would be.

"The kitchen and dining room will be larger than any ever built," he said. "We will fill it with friends and family."

"And our children?" she said.

Owen laughed. "Yes, many children."

Connie walked to the edge of a cliff. "And this will be the most special room of all."

"Which?" Owen said.

"The library. Filled with books and stories to enjoy each day. And a window right here so you can see the world."

Some people are born to do great things. Owen Reeder was born to *be* great. Some are given destinies they do not understand. His was to lead in love and return many to his father, to make sons and daughters of them all.

Epilogue

A world that becomes new does not leave behind every vestige of the old. Though the graves in the valley near the White Mountain were empty, the scars in the earth remained. The Dragon's body wasted away until it was only scales on the wind, but the scales stayed.

One scale, gray and withered and lighter than air, floated above the trees, past the cave of the fourth portal, and down into the valley. It danced on the wind until it came to rest on the surface of the water. Drifting, tossed by the undulating waves, it finally sank and slowly settled on a rock.

Fish, looking for insects or algae,

nibbled at but passed on the bitter scale. A crack appeared in the rock and soon ran the length of the oblong sphere. And every underwater creature of any kind quickly darted away, sensing evil.

The Wormling series is an allegory,
a story designed to make a point.
We hope you have learned something
about yourself from our tale, but let us
explain our reason for the telling.

Owen represents each of us—an
ordinary, seemingly insignificant person. What he doesn't realize at the
beginning is the same thing we often
forget—that if we have a relationship
with the King, we enjoy authority
given by him. We were designed by
him. Nothing happens by chance. Our
life is a unique tapestry woven by an
unseen hand.

We are also, whether we realize it or
not, engaged in a fierce battle between

good and evil, and it is our choice whether to pick up weapons and fight or do something else.

While this present world seems like all there is, a much bigger reality awaits. What we do in this life reaches into the next.

The duality of the characters in the story, such as Watcher and Constance, represents the split between our spiritual lives and our physical ones. However, as we see in the end, when we allow the King to make us whole, these two can come together beautifully as we were meant to be.

While there are obvious parallels to Jesus, God, the angels, Satan, and other biblical characters and themes, we admit that there are also many differences which leave our story merely that—a story. It is not meant to exactly reflect the Bible. For instance, the King has a wife (which God does not have), Owen makes mistakes (which Jesus doesn't do), and so on.

We are grateful that you have picked up this saga and hope you have enjoyed the adventure. May you be aware of the presence and power of the King in your life today.

Jerry B. Jenkins
Chris Fabry

ABOUT THE AUTHORS

Jerry B. Jenkins (jerryjenkins.com) is the writer of the Left Behind series. He owns the Jerry B. Jenkins Christian Writers Guild, an organization dedicated to mentoring aspiring authors. Former vice president for publishing for the Moody Bible Institute of Chicago, he also served many years as editor of *Moody* magazine and now serves on Moody's board of trustees.

His writing has appeared in publications as varied as *Time* magazine, *Reader's Digest, Parade, Guideposts,* in-flight magazines, and dozens of other periodicals. Jenkins's biographies include books with Billy Graham, Hank Aaron, Bill Gaither, Luis Palau, Walter Payton, Orel Hershiser, and Nolan Ryan, among many others. His books appear regularly on the *New York Times, USA Today, Wall Street Journal,* and *Publishers Weekly* best-seller lists.

Jerry is also the writer of the nationally syndicated sports-story comic strip *Gil Thorp*, distributed to newspapers across the United States by Tribune Media Services.

Jerry and his wife, Dianna, live in Colorado and have three grown sons and four grandchildren.

✦

Chris Fabry is a writer and broadcaster who lives in Colorado. He has written more than 50 books, including the RPM series and collaboration on the Left Behind: The Kids and Red Rock Mysteries series.

You may have heard his voice on Focus on the Family, Moody Broadcasting, or Love Worth Finding. He has also written for *Adventures in Odyssey* and *Radio Theatre*.

Chris is a graduate of the W. Page Pitt School of Journalism at Marshall University in Huntington, West Virginia. He and his wife, Andrea, have nine children, two dogs, and a large car-insurance bill.

RED ROCK MYSTERIES

#1 Haunted Waters

#2 Stolen Secrets

#3 Missing Pieces

#4 Wild Rescue

#5 Grave Shadows

#6 Phantom Writer

#7 Double Fault

#8 Canyon Echoes

#9 Instant Menace

#10 Escaping Darkness

#11 Windy City Danger

#12 Hollywood Holdup

#13 Hidden Riches

#14 Wind Chill

#15 Dead End

BRYCE AND ASHLEY TIMBERLINE are normal 13-year-old twins, except for one thing—they discover action-packed mystery wherever they go. Wanting to get to the bottom of any mystery, these twins find themselves on a nonstop search for truth.

CP0140

The Future Is Clear

Check out the exciting Left Behind: The Kids series